Steve Hussy worked in many bars for years before training to be a teacher. He taught for six years in colleges and universities, predominantly in the South-East of England.

Hussy formed Murder Slim Press in 2004. 'The Savage Kick' – MSP's literary magazine – has been one of the launching pads for best-selling authors Mark SaFranko and Tony O'Neill.

'The Savage Kick' has also published a number of established writers and artists, including: Dan Fante, Joe R. Lansdale, Jim Goad, Doug Stanhope, and Joe Matt.

When not busy editing or doing design work, Steve Hussy writes stories. His previous works include 'Steps' and numerous stories in magazines printed internationally.

NARCOLEPTIC
Copyright © 2006 Steve Hussy
All rights reserved
ISBN: 9798644384990

Narcoleptic is presented as a work of fiction and any likeness to any person living or dead is entirely coincidental.

10 9 8 7 6 5 4 3 2 1
First Printing

Cover and Interior Art © 2006 Steve Hussy

No part of this book may be used or reproduced in any manner whatsoever without written permission from the publisher, except in the case of quotations embodied in critical articles and reviews.

For all queries contact:
Murder Slim Press,
Sycamore Cottage,
Mill Road,
Burgh Castle, Norfolk.
NR31 9QS
United Kingdom

Published by Murder Slim Press 2006
www.murderslim.com

Printed in the UK by the MPG Books Group, King's Lynn.

Also by Steve Hussy:

Steps

The Savage Kick

"How helpless they all looked in the ugliness of sleep. A third of life spent unconscious and corpselike. And some, the great majority, stumbled through their waking hours scarcely more awake, helpless in the face of destiny.

"They stumbled down a dark alley toward their deaths. They sent exploring feelers into the light and met fire and writhed back again into the darkness of their blind groping."

William Lindsey Gresham, Nightmare Alley

"I told myself: 'Imagine you're drinking. Where is it predestined I won't drink?' So to be against what is predestined I must drink."

Tim Krabbé, The Vanishing

"I was born when she kissed me. I died when she left me. I lived a few weeks while she loved me."

Dorothy B. Sayers, In A Lonely Place

NARCOLEPTIC BYSTANDERS HUSSY

- NARCOLEPTIC -
by Steve Hussy

1

The light blasted Steve Hussy's eyes. He had been sleeping again. Each time he would wake with a jolt... his eyes stinging and his mouth dry.

The more he drank, the stranger his dreams became. He enjoyed the way his brain kept trying to attack him. He would ride each dream through to its end – always somewhere between conscious and semi-conscious.

Yet this time when he blinked he knew he was fully awake: "I'm in trouble, aren't I?"

Not necessarily.

"Hmm."

Would you like a drink?

"Vodka, thanks."

We don't serve spirits here.

"Hmm."

We do a lovely red wine if you're interested?

The barman handed over a large glass of Pinot Noir.

Hussy drained it, then said: "I suppose you want to hear it all?"

Isn't that what all barmen do?

Hussy breathed in, then exhaled fumes that tasted of iron. He put on his best tough guy voice and his pale blue eyes stared forward.

The glass was refilled, and he told his story...

2

He had been asleep for 12 hours that day.

The wind and rain pulsed outside. These sudden bursts and gusts of noise infuriated Hussy. He pulled the bedsheet over his head and sleep came after thirty minutes of frustration at the endless noise of a seemingly endless world.

People say they're dead to the world when they sleep, yet Hussy felt exhilaratingly alive. He yearned for each lengthy sleep.

Entire movie plots would play out for him. They entertained him so much more than reality.

That night the tale that stuck was basic: he was dreaming about flowers. A field filled with pansies, roses, marigolds, daisies, dandelions, fat fleshy lilies and more. They stretched out, chest high, as far as he could see. They were every shade of black and white. They provided a nice contrast with the sky, which was a cloudless blue.

Hussy waded through the flowers, and now and then he came across a flower that wasn't monochrome. A purple pansy. A red rose. A white daisy with a yellow centre. As he went along, he picked them and gathered them.

Now there was a pond, and he looked down at a single golden tadpole darting around. A magical creature. And then there was a beautiful pink water lily and it grew before his eyes. Hussy looked at it, smiled broadly and added it to his bouquet.

He drew a long sniff of the flowers. They smelt clearer and cleaner than reality.

Then his eyes and nose started to run, and he sneezed a dust-cloud of neon yellow pollen. He started to choke and cough: "Kha-kha-ha-ha-khhha-ha".

And then a loud ringing sound woke him up.

3

Hussy dragged the phone to his ear and it made clattering noises along the way. He hated the rise of mobile phones even more than the corded phone he had resolutely stuck by.

"HELLO? HELLO?" it said. The voice was far too loud so he held the receiver away from him.

"Wah?" Hussy wet his lips and tried again: "What?"

"IS THAT HUSSY?" It was male, deep at first but then it went up at the end of the sentence: "HUSS-EEEE?"

"Yeah," he groaned, "you can stop shouting now."

"THIS IS…" Hussy put his free hand over the earpiece to

muffle the voice: "Marcus."

"Urgh."

"'Fraid to say Rick's dead."

"Oh."

"He's been killed."

Hussy didn't say anything.

Marcus said: "Shot in the ol' noggin."

Hussy still didn't say anything.

Marcus eventually said: "You better come down an' have a look... We can talk more then."

"Uh-huh."

"It's not far. Just on the east road leading outta Yarmouth."

"I know where you mean."

"See you soon, boy." The voice hung up.

Hussy thought: "Boy?" as his right eye unpeeled with a pop and the left followed soon after.

He slapped himself across the face and felt it sting. He was probably awake. He had spent so much of his life asleep, it ceased to matter much.

The only surprise he felt about Rick Acton's death was how it may have happened. Acton was the equivalent of a time-bomb that would spew random numbers until it hit zero.

Hussy clambered out of bed and into a shirt, creased suit, baseball cap and some dirty black trainers. The lace snapped on one of them.

So Acton was dead. That meant he would be next.

Ah, well...

He felt his face. It wasn't shaved but it didn't matter. All he needed was a full head transplant.

He called for his favourite taxi... 0-8000-CABGUY.

"Olympia building, please."

The cabbie said: "Gimme five minutes, my friend."

"Thanks, Shubey."

"The turd shall guide me!" They laughed and he hung up.

The turd was a Walnut Whip on the top of the Olympia. It lit up at night as a glowing maroon testament to bad architecture. Great Yarmouth had been named by someone with a severe sense of irony...

Yarmouth was a mass of hotel rooms, drug deals, affairs, angry English, angry Polish, angry Portuguese. But Hussy knew that all of them were surrounded by water and occasional people of absolute beauty. Acton would have been killed anywhere. The location of it had as much importance as a green screen behind an actor.

Hussy wandered into the office, lifted up the blinds and glanced outside. It was dark, with only the faintest sliver of a moon. The small town was lit the wispy clouds sliding across the sky as they danced on a breeze.

He reached into the drawer and put his vodka into his back pocket.

Hussy carefully decanted booze into small plastic bottles

to avoid detection and to avoid breaking them when he passed out.

He put on his trenchcoat from the hatstand and then plopped on his hat. He ambled out of his office, through the reception room and out of the glass fronted door. It was marked "Acton & Hussy: Private Investigations."

The cab was waiting outside. Shubey was the only cab driver Hussy wanted to use repeatedly.

"HEY. MY MAN." It was Shubey, with his crinkled umber eyes and red checks that always sent out warmth. "You again?"

"Yep, me again."

"You keep my grand-kids in shoes!" Shubey laughed his beautiful laugh. His wife was a lucky woman...

"That makes me happy," Hussy said, and almost smiled.

"Where to, man?"

"East road outta here."

"I'm goin' to put the pedal to the metal for you, my man."

He roared off, and a couple of minutes in he said, a beaming smile reflected in the rear view mirror: "You know my son discovered the Tiktaalik roseae?"

Hussy looked confused: "Could you say that in English?"

Shubey thought for a second, then said: "It's the first fish-man." He smiled: "It proves we're all evolved from fish."

The concept made utter sense to Hussy: "That's great."

The cab kept swimming through the rainstorm.

Shubey moved his head gently back and forth as he said:

"Ya know he doesn't believe in God? Did I tell ya that before?"

"No, you didn't."

"It's ok," the cab swam onwards, "he's a beautiful son."

"He certainly sounds like one."

Shubey's looked at Hussy in the rearview mirror: "You look ill, man, you ok?

Hussy shut his eyes: "I don't know."

"Hey... Steve... STEVE!"

Hussy opened his eyes for a few seconds and said: "Please get me there."

"Don't worry, man," Shubey said, the wrinkles on his face forming into worry. "I'll get you wherever and whenever, ok?"

Hussy fell asleep yet again.

4

It was 2004 and life was a confounding flux for Steve Hussy.

Why couldn't he think in straight lines? His machine mind sent out signals erratically. He was a human glitch, flicking on and off with sudden electric pulses shocking his brain.

Yarmouth was just the same... a low rent, ersatz version of something bigger. Both comprised of a strange, thin surface covering something they never were and never could be.

But Hussy liked Yarmouth for that reason. No-one cared

about its chaos and everyone disappeared into its mediocrity.

Hussy loved the sensation of being invisible. He corrected the pace of his breath and slowed it down so he couldn't hear it in the silence of his bedroom. Then he perfected walking like a cat, padding his feet so calmly that no-one knew he was there.

Hussy was only twenty-six but he had already seen too much. It was the manner in which he might die that bothered him. Meeting Rick Acton – who provided him with a clean gun – was both soothing and horrific.

Acton was a strange human being, but who isn't? His ego was both strong and fragile, like a shard of glass.

Stake-outs were gruelling for Hussy. He was trapped with a glutton chomping away at greasy food and watching philanderous lives.

Acton asked: "Why don't you swear?"

He gave Rick a disgusted look... he could see the half-eaten food in Acton's mouth: "Why would I?"

"Anger..." Acton gulped down some lukewarm, takeaway coffee. "Pain..." Hussy could smell that it had been laced with cheap whisky. "Emotion..."

"It seems redundant."

"Don't you ever get so angry you need to..." he fought for words, "to release it all?"

That made Hussy smile: "That sounds like defecating."

Acton stared at him: "That's exactly what it is."

Hussy kept smiling and kept his eye on the door.

Acton glared and said: "SAY IT."

"Why?"

Prodding Hussy's shoulder, he said: "At least, say ****."

Hussy said: "Hmm," and took a long swig of vodka. It went down easy. His throat had already been burnt by drinking for so long. He felt nothing then, and it was a wonderful feeling.

5

Shubey nudged his arm: "Wake up, man."

"Uh?" Hussy stirred awake.

Shubey had parked the cab close to the scene of Acton's murder. It was now raining heavily.

Two police car lights and an ambulance's lights blazed into the air. Hussy liked the way they lit the raindrops.

Shubey nudged him again: "Rick's dead?"

Hussy stared blankly ahead: "Yeah."

"I'll wait for you, ok?"

"Ok," Hussy smiled at one of his two friends: "Thanks." He adjusted his hat and Shubey helped him out of the back seat, saying: "Look, man..."

"It's ok."

Hussy walked over and looked down at Acton's body. There were no crime scene signs and no crime scene tape. Just a dead man laying in the rain, staring up at the sky.

Hussy reached into his pocket and he took a longer slug of vodka. He know he would die soon, but any pain was constantly anaesthetised. He could wake with welts on his body, or covered in blood, and he barely felt anything.

When Hussy was awake, the booze numbed him. When he was asleep his narcolepsy did the same thing. A 50/50 split that had formed something like a life.

Acton's corpse made Hussy look closer, tilting his head as he did so. Acton had a big grin... even with a big black hole where the centre of his forehead used to be.

Acton's second wife had christened Rick as "Upside-down Face." Even when Acton did break open his lips, the result looked like a down-turned bone. Most of the time he had a look of abject misery. Everything else was a leer, a smirk, a lip curl...

"AMAZING, AIN'T IT?" The voice splashed over and stood next to Hussy.

The wind breathed in and out, carrying the sand and the cold, hail-like rain. It soaked and rippled the white sheet that was stuck to Acton's body.

"Yeah." Hussy tucked down his hat and tried to hide behind it.

"Worked with Rick for years, ain't never seen him smile once," Marcus said. "Took him to see the strippers. Knew he liked the ladies a lot cos he said so..."

Hussy's eyes started to hang and he went to the side of the road. He sat down on the grass verge, worried that he would fall asleep again. The wet permeated through his trousers and tugged at his backside. Ah, ah, it didn't matter...

Frank Marcus waddled over again. He was 6 foot high and increasingly wide. He wore a blue and white tent that flapped in the gale. "NOTHIN'!" Marcus went on, "A titchy little smirk, that's it!." His words rasped like a file, slow but sure: "Went out with a BANG! That's for sure."

"Ah," Hussy said, and tried to focus on staying awake.

Marcus had a purple face, purple nose, purple ears, three purple rolls of flab which connected the bottom of his purple mouth to his blue collar.

"Found anything?" Hussy asked.

"Ah... his wallet. Credit cards. Membership cards to his clubs. Coupla hundred in notes. Nuttin' else, 'fraid."

The murderer hadn't tried to make out it was a robbery. Someone with a bit of style and originality.

"No suicide note," Marcus added.

Hussy sighed: "There goes my theory."

"Theory?"

Hussy lifted himself up from the verge with a wet backside and a soggy brain.

Marcus went on: "What grandiose theory might that be?"

Hussy hated the way police – usually the dumbest of society – tried to use big words to seem important: "The one where he flings himself out of a car with a hole in his head."

That shut Marcus up for a few seconds, but after that

Marcus yawned and dragged it out with some ahh-ing noises as if he expected a round of applause at the end.

"Tired?" Hussy said, looking down at the way Acton's blood had merged with the rivulets of blood and rain.

"You should know," Marcus pantomimed another yawn as he waddled back to his car. His midget partner with meerkat eyes greeted him. Cops were paid to strategically look, investigate, sleep, ignore, eat, excrete, urinate and fail.

Now he was alone, Hussy looked around fully.

He saw faint marks in the mud where Acton had been thrown from the car. They were in the process of being washed away, but there were clearly no skid-marks. The sheet did as good a job as anything thin, wet and white does. Hussy peeled it off.

Acton was dressed in an open, brown overcoat and a white, now mostly brown, shirt. He was wearing dirty black trousers and shoes. He'd got dressed in a hurry or had bad hand-eye co-ordination because the buttons on the shirt weren't lined up right. He was laying on his side, and his right arm was bent wrongly. Like his left ankle, it had been broken. He had a large deep gash in his chin, but there was almost no blood.

His face was old and tired but there was that rictus smile on Rick's whitewashed face. The car lights emphasised the thick black lines around his mouth and forehead. The entry wound was small and round. The skin around it was burnt. The rain had mostly washed away the a lot of his blood and his small brain.

Hussy crouched, head down, and watched the rain trickle off the brim of his fedora. They were the only tears he could muster. He drew the sheet over Rick's body and the face, but Acton still smiled through it at the black sky.

Marcus fidgeted and then came over again. He dug his own little hole in the ground with his shoe and he fiddled with his truncheon. He started to whistle. Then he stopped: "Well, boy, um..."

"He been here long?"

Marcus burst into life: "Got here meself after the first guys here found the wallet and they knew I knew Rick. They'd got the call at the station from a motorist, y'see? An' then..."

"Get a name?"

"Nah. Male, probably young, they said. Don't get many who submit their names these days. The guys called me cos I was on patrol and y'know Rick ain't popular no more so they said they'd like it if I could handle it."

Hussy blinked his eyes.

Marcus rambled on: "Then me and Rob came, soon as we could."

"How long?"

"Well, um, prob'ly... well." Somehow he turned even more purple. "Must be only 'bout coupla hours or so."

"TWO HOURS?"

"I 'spect there's another homicide somewhere in town, y'know." He had a nervous chuckle. His sixty-something chins and moustache shook: "Shouldn't be long now. He ain't going nowhere, anyway."

Hussy knew he hated cops, but he couldn't pinpoint why. All he knew was every encounter with a cop solidified that nebulous thought: "So Acton festers away and the stuff for forensics washes away? YOU'RE A MORON."

"Don't get at me, Hussy." Marcus poked a podgy finger at him. Then he withdrew it when Hussy didn't flinch.

"Like anyone who dishes out casual insults," Hussy said, "you can't take the truth yourself."

"Look, after Rick quit I stuck by him, OK? Just me." He was now the colour of beetroot. "All those things he said... Crazy and lonely, even when he HAD a woman." His head wobbled from side to side.

Some headlights blazed down the road. They turned around. The meat wagon had arrived, going a steady 25 but still veering from side to side.

Marcus said: "Here comes the cavalry." Another inane comment to add to his collection.

"I'm going," Hussy said. He walked down the road and his shoe got stuck in the mud. Another dramatic exit ruined...

Marcus laughed.

Hussy shoved the shoe back on and tucked in the lace again. Then he walked back and flicked Marcus' policeman's hat off with his forefinger.

Marcus said "WHAT?" as the hat fell down. His red rug fell

down with it. Moments of sheer beauty were few and far between for Hussy, but this was one of them.

Marcus' head was completely bald except for two strips of double sided tape with a couple of strands of red fibre on them. Fat drops of rain fell on his head and trickled down.

Everyone else called him by his surname, but Hussy knew his true first name: "See you next time, Francisssssss..."

Marcus steamed, the heat rising from the anger and rain. His fat head was like a purple pool ball ready to be racked up.

"Now," Hussy said, "that is beautiful." He looked down at Marcus and smiled.

Marcus' mouth flapped but the words didn't come.

Hussy walked back to Shubey's taxi. Outside the door, he reached into his pocket, fumbled past his gun, and he took out his Modafinil and a tablet of speed. He washed them down with the vodka. He didn't want to fall asleep here.

All the pettiness of life had damaged him, but how many people were pristine? Everyone was scarred by the horror of life, death and love. Aside from food and water, they were the only things that mattered.

Hussy's only strategy had been to breeze through life in the best way he could, floating on a current of red wine and vodka.

Until now, it had worked reasonably well.

6

Hussy knew he was strange, but he had become accustomed to his strangeness. He had an unnatural hatred of obese people, the smell of coffee, TV programmes, the limpness of modern music and the callousness of organised religions.

The barman looked at him and smiled the vacuous smile of someone who could accept these things and not worry.

But when Hussy computed all of his issues – in bed at night, sitting in a cab, in this bar – he knew his true hatred was simply his own life.

Would you like another drink?

"Always," Hussy smiled and hacked a drinker's cough: "Judge not, lest yet lest be judged."

Hussy finally grinned at the nonsense of it all.

But how did you feel?

Hussy said: "Wet."

The bartender withheld a sigh, and drained off a glass of wine himself. Even he was getting tired.

Emotionally...

"Look, we're almost in the same business. You can see everything at anytime."

But not inside.

"But you know the answer."

Yes. But not why.

"You need to look harder."

Some watch, but when you can access everything only certain things appeal.

"So what do you want to see?"

The truth.

7

Hussy nestled in the warmth of the taxi seat.

Shubey said: "What happened?"

"Ah, you know…"

"Rick?" He revved away from the scene of the crime.

"Yeah…"

"I saw the police lights," Shubey said, "and the meat wagon…"

"Yeah."

"You ok?" Another gentle look in the backview mirror.

"I will be," then he paused before saying, "or not."

Hussy thought about the movement of life as sleep came. It was as quick as Shubey speeding through the streets.

Life was alien in so many ways. He thought about how small Acton actually was. Even puffed up by the water soaking into his body. What had Acton ever been?

Being a narcoleptic had its advantages, and it gave Hussy's stomach and mind enough time to fully digest Acton's death.

Shubey woke him up when they arrived at the apartment

building. He helped him out of the taxi and up the stairs.

"Shubey..."

"No need to say anything, man. Get yourself dry, ok?"

Shubey left, and the Yale lock on the door clicked across.

The memory of the first time he met Rick flared as Hussy laid face down on the office couch.

It was cold and wet. The trees were dropping multi-coloured fire. The wind took the fire and spread it around until it died on the pavement. Then it merely laid in a sad brown mash.

Hussy was already angry and insular. He'd been to university and studied films. He'd had a girlfriend before she jetted off around the world with a new guy. She had invited him to travel with him, and he'd declined. Stupid, stupid...

He'd been scared to commit to difference, a situation he regretted every day. So he continued to work in the same bar that had funded his university course. It was at a holiday camp. The punters were only be there for a week at a time, and that appealed to him. The customers were films too – snapshots of lives and conversations that had a finite end after they left.

He thought about the beauty of the free booze there, and took a long slug of vodka from the remnants of the innocent looking bottle in his pocket.

Over time, he had become bored of the regulation drunks. Their rambling stories and their tenuous relationship to the truth. Over time, the best material ended up repeating, just spoken from different mouths. They became progressively more ugly and stupid. Numbing himself with booze was an occupational hazard that he had fallen into head-first.

The alcoholism had started in the bar, but the voyeurism had always existed. He watched and listened, permanently outside and impossible to pin down. He'd been offered the chance of becoming a Film Studies' teacher from a previous tutor who was quitting to become a writer.

The thought had scrambled his nerves. What if he fell asleep during a lesson?

Instead of hiding in the background, he would be front and centre. He knew the thoughts would pound away like hammers. He knew he would have to drink even more to survive it all.

So Hussy stayed put, reading books and Wanted Ads during the quiet times at the bar.

When he saw the words PRIVATE DETECTIVE WANTED, they stood out in glorious 3D.

Here there would be difference.

The advert went on: EXPERIENCE NOT NEEDED. CALL RELPENO & ACTON: P.I'S. CALL 0-800-PIGUYS.

Well, ok... He broke out into one of his rare smiles.

8

Above all, Hussy thought it would fun. A story to perk up

his mundane life. As a goof, he bought a fedora and wore some dark glasses. He developed his noir character beforehand and practised in the mirror like Travis Bickle.

The door was marked *Relpeno & Acton: Private Investigations* and it opened out into a small office.

A woman sat cross-legged behind a desk in the middle of the room. She was blabbing into a phone and lazily tapping on a keyboard her free hand. She didn't stop when Hussy walked in. She just peered around the computer and winked.

"...then Bobby tells Tommy that, you know, he isn't going to stand for this anymore, so I'm like, ohmigod, don't hit him or nothing..."

She was maybe 22, with blonde hair halfway down her back. Her big red lips flapped away quickly and easily. She had an open desk and her red micro-skirt was hitched almost all the way up. The top of her sheer stockings showed, little brown lattices. The voyeur came out in Hussy once again...

She was certainly American, so why was she here?

"...but then Tommy says somethin' like 'You think I care?' and then he walks off, so I'm just standing there and Bobby's smiling but I think that maybe I like Tommy more..."

Hussy crossed his arms, sat back and listened.

"...and then..." There was the click of the door behind her. She slammed the phone down and started typing with both hands.

Hussy watched a short, chubby, older man in a white shirt

step out of his office.

"This gentleman," Erica's voice dripped with sarcasm, "has just arrived, Mr. Acton."

"Thankyou for buzzing that through so quickly..." He held a lengthy look at Erica before he turned and said: "You Hussy?"

"Yeah."

"Great name." More sarcasm, this time it was pointed.

"Thanks," he glared at Acton, "I was born blessed."

"Funny." Acton turned, and in the doorway he paused and said: "Lose the sunglasses."

Hussy put them in his pocket as he passed Erica. He had no luck at catching what her breasts were like. He was shallow, but the deeper pool of water in his thoughts was growing.

Acton took a seat behind the desk. The office was dark and dingy and smelled of sweat. Hussy's chair was low... a ridiculous power game.

He noticed Acton had a big forehead. A big target. It wasn't that his hair was receding – although it looked dumb perched up there – it was just his forehead was out of proportion with the rest of his head.

Hussy passed him his curriculum vitae. Acton looked at it for a second, screwed it up, threw it at a bin in the corner. It rimmed out.

He interlaced his fingers on the desk and stared at Hussy. Hussy stared back. Acton was pasty faced, and he looked like a peeled potato with a little brown leaf on top.

"So. You want to be a private eye?"

No. A teacher. "Yeah."

He drew out a pencil and started writing.

"Steve Hussy, hey?"

"We did that."

"Still love that name." He said the next line deadpan: "As you know, we have an opening."

"Yeah."

"My partner just died."

"Oh."

"Natural causes. Heart... Too much booze," Acton said. "Do you drink?"

"Yeah."

"Good. What makes you think you can do this job, boy?"

"A degree in Psychology," which was only half a lie...

"That doesn't mean much."

"I know law."

"That could help. Sometimes. You married?"

"No."

"Girlfriend? Children?"

"No and no."

"Do you have any charm?"

"Some."

"Do you mind working late?"

"No."

"Do you know private eyes aren't so popular?"

"I do now."

"Do you care?"

"No."

"Every now and then you have to punch someone or be attacked." Acton narrowed his eyes when he said that: "Does that bother you?"

"No."

"Do you think you're tough?"

"Enough."

"Do you think you could take me?"

Hussy knotted his eyebrows and looked at Acton. He was below average height and paunchy. The three shirt-buttons straining over Acton's belly were hard workers.

Hussy was 6'2", thin with broad shoulders and big hands that were ideal for fighting: "Yeah."

"It says here you got," and Acton smiled as he traced the word with his fingers, "nar-co-lep-sy."

Hussy shrugged: "I fall asleep a lot."

"You don't think that's a major problem?"

"I can't drive, but I can get around."

Acton now rubbed his left forefinger around his eye: "You need a crash helmet on the streets?"

"I have a hard head," Hussy sighed, "and the meds have got better over time."

They stared at each other for twenty long seconds, with neither of them blinking.

Acton leaned back on his chair. Hussy felt like pushing it so it would topple over.

Acton said: "You have a lot to learn."

"Yeah."

"I think I can work with you," and he reached out a clammy hand.

"Hmm."

Acton said: "I can be some kind of... mentor... to you."

Hussy let out a slow breath, barely audible: "Ahhh..."

"You act like a pussycat," Acton smiled, "and I can teach you to be a doberman."

Hussy stifled a laugh.

Acton clearly thought he was Mike Hammer.

Hussy thought he was Philip Marlowe.

Loser and Loser were open for business.

9

The memories flowed into a dream as he laid on the futon in his office, still unable to move.

This time he remembered the light. It blasted his eyes. Indistinct shapes formed behind a mist. The mist was full of bright colours. He could smell wet grass. A warm breeze brushed his face. Vertical brown shapes reared up around him. He heard some birds sing but it was like a repetitive tape recording.

Hussy tried to move. No luck. His feet were one with the earth. His toes felt like roots, reaching for water. Everything kept redrawing around him, making his stomach churn.

He closed his eyes but as he did, the screaming started. The birds stopped signing. The screaming became louder.

Rick Acton. It was his voice, he knew it was.

He kept his eyes shut, but then the screams got nearer.

His eyes opened. He scrunched his eyes and the world slowly went into sharp focus. Trees, leaves and, oh no, Acton...

He was in front of Hussy, rolling about. He had bruises, some blood. There were holes in his body, with grass quickly growing through them.

Hussy tried to move... to help or run. But his feet stayed frozen. Rick stopped screaming. As he watched, long green blades burst through a hole in Acton's forehead.

Acton said " Ah," and smiled his grey, phantom smile.

The grass looked pretty as it waved in a breeze.

A woman laughed. Another bad tape recording. It didn't sound so bad, though.

Hussy looked at himself and he'd turned red. A big, slimy, dripping, red dude.

What little was left of his mind tried to reconstruct the dream into something else. Francesca appeared in the mist, wearing a ivory silk camisole. Her body kept shifting – short and busty, or tall and lithe – but her face remained clear. She wet her lips and opened them: "Are you ok?"

He heard the ticking of a clock, but it was something more like heels on a floor.

Francesca's subtle perfume drifted into him.

He wanted to stay asleep but feel that smell forever.

10

Another glass of red wine was in front of Hussy. He was now sipping it and he felt like himself again.

"I remember everything," he said.

Why?

"I wish I didn't... it was after the narcolepsy kicked in."

He felt life was so eye-watering dull it was a shock that everyone didn't fall asleep. A life of idle gossip, whining about partners and friends and family before plastering on a fake grin.

Faint glimpses of truth and wonder were only seen through steel bars of boredom and normality.

Hussy said: "I had this bat-faced doctor with little teeth who called them hypnagogic hallucinations". He shrugged again: "Microsleeps, cataplexy, excessive daytime sleepiness."

Peter was frustrated again: *How do they make you FEEL?*

"Look, with my stupid dreams," Hussy said, "I'll give you the edited highlights. The ones with the freaky stuff. I reckon we've got the time."

We certainly do.

11

Hussy heard the sound of Fran's heels pattering across the bare floorboards of the reception.

"STEVE," and then she said it louder: "ARE YOU OK?"

Hussy got one eye open, tried to twist the top half of his body around to look at the neon clock on his bedside table. He went too far and landed on the floor with a bump.

He said: "Ow."

The bat-faced doctor called this "sleep paralysis." His brain was awake but his body wasn't.

Now her voice was shouting through the door: "STEVE?!"

He could feel a bump on the back of his head swell. He managed to get his lips moving and slurred: "Urrrrrrr, fffine."

"You don't sound fine."

"Fffiles."

"Files? Have you dropped something?"

"Yeah." Hussy's mouth loosened up. "I'm OK." He was flushed and he had trouble lying to her. It was only with her...

"Are you sure?"

"Sure I'm sure."

"Hold on. I'll come in and give you a hand." The doorknob slowly turned.

"NO!" He screamed then toned it down: "No, no, really... I'm fine."

The doorknob stopped turning.

"Ok."

"Can you make me..." Ow. Ow. Ow. "A cup of coffee. In Rick's office. That would be great."

"Well, OK. I'll be in reception." Another pause, maybe another pout... the way she jutted out her chin was such beauty to him. "Um, see you soon."

Pitter-patter, pitter-patter. Click went the door as it opened. Pitter-patter. Click went the door as it shut. Pitter-patter, pitter-patter. Click went the kettle.

The thin curtains let through diffused morning rays.

Hussy decided not to sleep naked any more.

He had the heart for it, but not the body.

12

Hussy was all too aware of how he looked. The greatest compliment about him had been: "You have the saddest eyes I've ever seen."

His nose was too big and sniffed for trouble. His ears stuck out and his face was a little too long. He was too tall for his weight too.

His arms woke up and he fumbled for clothes. His head throbbed as the sleep paralysis wore off.

He counted the ceiling tiles until the throbbing stopped. It didn't take long - 94.

He lifted his head, and grabbed it to check it still worked. He looked at the red neon on the clock. It was 8.50am.

Francesca was early again.

He made it to his feet using the bed, then staggered into the bathroom and the shower.

In 15 minutes he had showered and shaved. He put on his last fresh shirt and the still damp suit. He stuck on his other fedora, brim down, and stepped out.

A mug of coffee sat on the burled walnut desk in Rick's office. He made it to the window and hoisted up the blinds.

The light hit him. He'd got too accustomed to the dark. He adjusted the blinds so thin streaks of light shone through onto the wall. He smiled at the play of light and dark.

He had a sip of the beautiful coffee, washing down his narcolepsy meds but avoiding another dose of speed. The sense of mundanity hit him again as he looked around. He took a swig of the cheap grain vodka he found in Rick's bottom drawer.

He logged into Rick's laptop, and sat thinking what an accomplished voyeur Rick was. That had made his password easy to guess: *"Francesca."*

Rick had said: "The only difference between a pervert and an amateur is opportunity and skill." Acton had smiled after the word "skill."

Acton's pornography was not difficult to find. The women looked young but they were simply young looking, tall and blonde... Brianna Banks, Jenna Jameson, Teagan Presley.

There were other – professionally shot – photosets of young looking blondes that Hussy didn't recognise.

The women looked like smiling, happy people. Nothing was illegal, nothing contained violence, but it still troubled Hussy. Why did porn peddle women in schoolgirl outfits? It nauseated him, just as schoolgirl themed hen-nights were the female version of self-destruction.

Fran was sitting in the reception room at her desk, past the glass door. An open desk, side-on view. Oh, Fran...

She was wearing black knee boots and an almost knee length skirt. There was the merest glimpse of her beautiful brown thighs. They glowed.

Had she put moisturiser on them? Her skin was so flawless, she was everything, she was a true woman.

Hussy passed out onto the keyboard, his forehead typing "iuhtvitgeih."

Fran shouted: "STEVE!" from the other side of the glass and he woke up again.

He raised his coffee and said too loudly: "I'M FINE."

Fran cocked her head to one side and breathed out: "Steve. It's ok."

It wasn't. Hussy was in deep trouble. Even her breathing sent his thoughts racing, and he was too dumb to figure out why.

He didn't know whether it was love, pity, care, anger, or a combination of all four.

13

Hussy had hired Fran 10 months earlier.

It was a Spring afternoon. The sun wasn't shining, and the birds were hiding from the wind.

Erica had dropped out. It'd been dragging on for a while before that. Her coffee always tasted like mud and her typing was always bad. But by the end, things skewed into horror.

Erica had lost a lot of weight over a few months. She was scrawny, pinched. She kept on with her teeny-tops and belt-skirts. Big green eyes with pin-point irises stared and twitched from yellowed sclera.

She'd lost control of something. Something must have triggered it. She was popping, injecting, snorting, sniffing, eating, drinking, smoking, inhaling, ramming, dropping something.

Hussy hated the disintegration but Acton seemed to revel in it. He continued to stare at her body and sweat profusely.

Her destruction gave him power: "Type these up." And Erica would slowly set to work, blinking and trying to focus.

On the days she wasn't there, he'd say just the same to Hussy. "Type these up." He could do it in twenty minutes but he feigned it for two hours as some sort of revenge.

The last time Erica showed up, she had been in the toilet for an hour.

Acton oozed over towards to bathroom door, watched by Hussy, and Jack shouted: "HEY, ERICA."

She shouted back: "WHAT?"

"WHAT'RE YOU DOING IN THERE?"

"COME IN. I WON'T BE LONG."

Acton went in, and Hussy stayed where he was.

He heard a muffled: "Hiya, big boy"

Then Hussy still watched more as he dragged her out by her arm. He only stood up then, and moved towards them.

Acton said: "If I wanted ribs I'd go to a barbeque."

Hussy said: "Rick..."

"HEY. You're NASTY to me." She grinned at Acton and blanked Hussy. "You want some action. It's FUN." She giggled.

Hussy shoved Acton against the wall. "Stop it."

Erica laid on the ground and said: "I'LL WORK IT, BABIES."

Acton puffed-up and glared at Hussy and Erica. This idiotic barrel-chested and big-gutted semi-human: "Are you gonna puke first or do you want me to?"

Erica stood up at that, suddenly alert, then ran into the cubicle. She shut the door behind her and the lock slammed shut.

Hussy kept standing as Rick whistled a happy little tune. It kept out most of the noise of her vomiting.

Hussy tried to think of reasons to not close his hand around Jack's neck.

Instead he watched Acton sneer, then start to sing like a bad Charles Aznavour impersonator: "Sheeeee... may be the face I can't forget... A trace of pleasure or regret... Maybe my treasure or the price I have to pay... Sheeee may be the song that summer sings, maybe the chilling autumn winds...."

Hussy clenched his fists and the puking sounds stopped.

Hussy waited. Acton waited, then he knocked on the cubicle: "HEY."

Nothing.

"HEY!" Louder this time. "GET ON WITH IT."

Still nothing. Acton bashed a fist on the door.

Hussy pushed him aside again and looked under the door's little gap. Two high heeled soles looked back and there was effluent on the floor.

Hussy knocked the door open with his shoulder, and Erica was laying there... but she wasn't here anymore. He went over to her and brushed the hair from her face. It was coated in vomit and her eyes had rolled back.

"She's pulled an Elvis," Rick said, as he loomed over Hussy. There must have been something like a smile in his head, although his face – as ever – didn't show it. "Stupid ****."

Hussy didn't know why he didn't kill him right then.

Acton met Hussy's look as he turned around and glared at him. "Oh stop it," Jack said. "What gives you the right to act all high and mighty?"

14

Poor Erica was taken away, and on the afternoon after the funeral, Acton said: "We need a new secretary, huh?"

Acton let Hussy figure it out. He hated computers, whereas Hussy knew the ropes.

Hussy posted an ad online. Three replied. One spelt woman "wimmin" and wrote in crayon. One liked "killing Private Dicks." Ho-ho-ho.

Hussy invited the only serious one in, but the salary was so meagre he couldn't expect much. This was during the height of Blair's Britain... mass employment and pseudo-cool-just-left-of-centre existence. Scummy little jobs like Hussy's were increasingly redundant.

Hussy's eyelids had sagged shut then lurched open when there was a polite knock at the door. He didn't look up at first, but murmured: "Ye-ah?"

"Sorry... Hello." Now a snort from her too: "Are you ok?"

He lifted his head and the negative waves in his brain disappeared and were filled by her. He had the unerring feeling he'd seen and heard her before.

Her face glowed mocha, her cheeks were red and so was her nose. She sneezed, and her nose did an impersonation of a tap, but she recovered with a tissue. Her semi-straightened, yet still curly, afro hair sat on her shoulders, flecked with lighter tones. The sight was staggering, more so than any of his dreams.

Hussy's dumb mouth opened. He became scared he wouldn't be able to move. The narcolepsy mightn't be able to handle her. He tried hard to concentrate: "Miss Dawn?"

"Sorry," she said. Her mouth puckered and her honey coloured eyes flared, "iz my nose."

Words caught in his throat, then: "It's a lovely nose."

She sniffed, smiled and said: "'Ullo, Mr. Hussy."

She had the job.

She wasn't conventionally beautiful, but then true beauty isn't. The same rules apply for being conventionally intelligent.

Hussy slowly rotated his neck and opened and shut his eyes: "Can you sit down, please?"

Her breasts weren't too out of proportion to the rest of her. She was tall, maybe 5-9 in her low heels, 5-7 without.

Fran grinned: "Yes, I can. I learned how to one time."

Everything about her flowed. A willow tree hasn't set out to look good, it just is. It finds it's own form and then you admire it. Fran's jacket gently expanded around her bust and tapered at the waist. Rare, rare, rare. Her skirt was tight at the hips. The grey fabric hugged them close. It gripped around her thighs before it cut off above the knee.

He desperately wanted to slide out the vodka from the drawer and negate his firework thoughts.

Francesca stopped blowing her nose and sat opposite him, smiling with true intelligence.

She pulled out her CV and passed it to him. His arms felt

shaky. Another symptom he hated – cataplexy – wobbly muscles during stress, excitement.

Hussy garbled: "Fank you…"

She said: "Well, thank you." And she took another sniff.

He focussed on moving his mouth correctly: "You must be Miss Dawn."

"'Ullo!" Her cheeks rose, her lips stretched, those white teeth popped out. Her little nose crinkled. A car dealer would've killed for that smile. This woman could not lie with a smile like that. "Pleased to meet-ya, Mr. Hussy."

Hussy looked at her CV with steadying hands. Nicely presented. She was 26, a year older than him. She had been to a decent uni and studied American Literature with a dissertation on Kerouac. She'd worked as a secretary for 4 years, at the D.A.'s. Hmm… that glorified and corrupt arbiter of justice.

Hussy kept his head down: "Did you enjoy the D.A.'s?"

"It waz OK, but I needta move on. An' den dis came up." She had a nice voice with the faintest of a London accent.

Hussy looked at her then: "What was it like with Wilson?"

"You know 'im?"

Of course he did. He often had to deal with the D.A. Wilson was another huge, grating voyeur. "I supply his do-nuts."

"DREEEEE…" She was smiling. A strange throaty noise was building up, getting higher.

"Are you OK?"

She swallowed and stopped making the noise. "Yes, he

certainly does like iz do-nuts," she said, through some muffled snorts. "An' he certainly likes to," then her face changed, "investigate women."

Ah. "I'm sorry."

"Iz ok," she grinned again, "I'm good at dealing wiv snake hands."

Hussy was already in love, and his leg shuddered more as he said: "You pretty good at coffee?"

"I think so," her nose twitched to the left. "Wilson drank enough of it. Iz a wonder he didn't pee all day." She giggled at that too and that was as sublime as her voice.

"YOU'RE HIRED," Hussy said, all too loudly. She could do so much better than his place...

"Oh. Fanks. Um. I can type too, y'know." She sniffed a little: "Use computers. All dat jazz."

"Great."

Francesca looked up and flashed her smile. "I can start tomorrow if you'd like me to..."

15

10 months on and Hussy still couldn't get used to her smile. He would smile back, forgot everything, and feel like a rabbit in the headlights.

"Morning," Fran said, "And how are you today?"

He struggled to control the twitching in his legs, even though he'd drank half of a bottle of vodka beforehand: "Ah."

Her pink lips narrowed along with her eyes: "What's going on?"

"I've got something to tell you."

"Hey, that's a song..." She smiled: "Am I getting a raise?"

"Not exactly."

"Damn."

"Rick's dead."

"Oh." She looked a little stunned. Not exactly upset, but who could blame her? "How?"

"Someone shot him in the head."

"When?"

"This morning."

She sat down as the shock hit her. She said: "Do they know who did it?"

Hussy scratched his fedora: "Could be gangsters..."

"Gangsters?"

"You know," even Hussy thought it was unlikely, "the mob?"

"I didn't know there was a mob around here."

"Well, I'm pretty sure there is." He was fumbling for words again. "The shot in the head fits."

"Why would they kill Rick?"

"Maybe he got on their nerves?"

Francesca was starting to piece together the previous

day: "He didn't leave here during the day, then he stayed at home all night with Cartman."

Cartman was the nickname for Acton's latest wife, and Hussy knew that Acton had lied about staying with her.

The previous night, with a leer, Rick had told him he was going to a strip club. Hussy didn't want to make that known yet. So he said: "It's difficult to work out who killed someone you hardly knew." It was also difficult to care, when there's nothing other than misguided duty as motivation. He asked: "Can you contact anyone who might've seen him after he left last night?"

"Who?"

"I don't know. Start with Cartman..." He corrected himself: "Jenny." Acton didn't have a family. There was just his wife and ex-wife, both of which weren't cut out for killing. "Can you get onto the police again? Find out what they have. Please."

"OK," she said, "I'll use my natural charm."

"I'm going into his office to look for," Hussy almost smiled at the lunacy of the next word, *"clues."*

"C'mon," she poked his arm, "you're smart..."

He smiled and tried to walk like Robert Mitchum as he went into Acton's office.

16

Hussy's aloofness was nothing compared to how Acton

Narcoleptic

had reacted to Fran being hired.

He had burst in with an oily leer and whisky stinkbreath. "You better have hired that one." Acton's eyes were almost three quarters open. It was the most excited Hussy would ever seen him. At least while Acton was still alive...

Hussy shrugged: "Now I know why your name is first."

"She was STACKED. Did you see her...?" He made a large cupping movement with his hands in front of his chest.

Hussy shut his eyes: "She's a good worker."

"Ooh, baby," and now he was drooling onto his two day old face fuzz. "I don't normally go for nig-nogs, but..."

Hussy's nostrils flared wide and his chin set: "DON'T."

"Well..." He looked idiotic standing there in his little pale pink suit. His gut and his scrawny legs created something like a tiny flamingo. Acton stood up as straight as he could manage. "Never mix business and pleasure," he said. "That's what I say."

"I'm sure she wants you too..."

Acton's thoughts rattled around and: "Shut up, boy," eventually came from his mouth.

"You can still leer at her," said a hypocrite.

"No harm in looking, boy. No harm at all."

"Yeah," the hypocrite said.

"You did good, Sleepy." Acton slithered off, leaving his blend of body odour, cheap alcohol and unwashed clothes.

Hussy heard the familiar sound of him slamming the door into the toilet. No wonder Hussy was scared of that damned room.

Acton was a coward in many respects. Addicted to his wife, but desperate to show individuality. Without her to control him he was, well, dead by the side of a road...

Fortunately, Fran stayed as eye candy that Acton never touched. But she was someone to shout at for coffee or typewriting. Fran was his PG-rated office girlie show, and Rick regarded her with that vile face that never cracked open.

Maybe that's why he couldn't smile. You can't fake a smile that looks good. A good actor can make you believe a smile because they create the emotion behind it in their head. But it still wasn't real, and Hussy could see it in their eyes.

Hussy found it difficult to like anyone who doesn't show any emotion... but it was difficult to dislike them too. What was Acton? A sleaze? A man driven by justice? A lunatic?

Acton did his job well. He split 50/50 in money and work. He shouted at Fran too much – probably because detectives did that on TV... but Fran could give as good as she got.

"This coffee smells like ****!"

Hussy's eyes flicked up, and he watched Fran prowl to Acton's desk like a panther. She said: "So does your backside," and then she leaned in ever further, "although the toilet smells a little... hmm... salty?"

Rick's face swelled up, but no words – unlike other things – would come.

Hussy started laughing and Fran poked her tongue out at

him as she walked away.

He watched her diligently type at her desk as she giggled.

17

Hussy plonked his backside on Acton's chair. He figured his jeans would shield him from too much contamination.

The calculator in his mind set to action.

A year ago, a woman came in and asked them to look into the death of her son. This was the only murder they ever investigated. The rest of their jobs were trivial garbage-raking.

The kid had been shot in the forehead too... a ghastly version of what happened to Rick.

The poor kid was 16, and the mother was just 32. She was too inexperienced to work out why the police had dropped the case. They said – through the press – that they couldn't find out anything.

Acton and Hussy found out everything in 4 days.

A police ballistics report had been accidentally-lost-on-purpose but found in a bin. The lab guy who typed the report was fake stunned, of course. The kid had been shot by a rare – and solely – police issue handgun.

On threat of being exposed, the lab guy (who is still happily working away) gave them a description of the cop involved. Acton knew him. The guy was called Stuart Bishop.

They went to see him and Bishop was in his flat. He'd almost finished the bottle of vodka that sat next to his filthy armchair. Bishop told his little tale, anaesthetised by his booze.

"So, I waz so drunnnk an' th' kid jus' wouldn't shut his mouth an' my head waz like... poundin'... Just deliver the..." and he paused: "package and shut up. So I turns 'round an' shoots 'im. POOF as 'is head went PLURP. Damn deadeye. Ya should've seen da blood." Then he laughed, he LAUGHED...

Hussy cracked down on Bishop's skull with his right hand. They dragged him into Acton's car, and drove the unconscious Bishop to the much bigger Police Station in Norwich. Once out of the small town logjam, rusty gears could be forced into action.

They played back the recording of the confession from tape, kept the copy of that tape made on the drive in, and of course Bishop confessed. His only explanation as to why the kid was in his room was to "deliver the post." He got 5 years – diminished responsibility, unpremeditated...

Hussy fumed. What thoughts were going through the kid's head? Death was never instantaneous. What was there for his last seconds?

Hussy hid in his office and watched Acton almost smile as the kid's mother handed over their payment. She was grateful and tearful. But Acton and Hussy had, merely, done their job.

Acton had felt the same about the kid as how Hussy felt about Acton being shot in the head.

Empty but with the need to fill that gap with something.

18

The hypocrisy of it all infuriated Hussy and, again, he reflectively scratched at his head through his fedora.

He asked Peter: "Why are you doing this?"

You know why.

Hussy almost smiled, despite the fresh tear-stains on his face: "Why do you have to be so..." ten words were tied on the end of tongue, before he selected the right one: "...elusive?"

Peter refilled the glass of wine, and smiled the smallest and saddest of smiles: *You were. You are.*

Hussy drained the glass of wine and said: "Toilet?"

There.

Hussy could feel his cheeks reddening in the stainless steel toilets. He urinated, carefully washed his hands, and averted looking at himself into the mirror. He hated his pale pink skin and the way his cheeks would glow at the slightest emotion.

But then the wine kicked in and he felt human again.

He knew he was ready to go.

19

Back in the now-deceased Acton's office, Hussy turned on the light.

It was the largest office, but with the same desk near the

back of the room, the same desk chair, a slightly wider and blinded window. Acton used to say: "The only good reason to open a window is to get a better aim."

Something knotted inside Hussy. The sense of being an intruder was the thing he hated about being a private detective. Of course, that formed most his lousy job...

He'd noticed Acton was private about his office. The longest time Hussy had spent in there was when he was interviewed. After being hired, clients were met in Hussy's office and only then after they'd been processed through reception.

The floorboards creaked like Rick was trying to tell him something. The walls were grey but filled with some pictures of boxers with skinny leather gloves and bright red trunks. There was another framed photo of Rick in a police uniform. He looked young and proud with his hand on his truncheon.

Hussy checked behind them all.

Nothing.

There was a two-year-old calendar adjacent to Acton's desk. July was up... a staggeringly beautiful, willowy woman with pale brown skin. It said – in gold embossed writing – *"Saskia."*

He flicked through the page of the calendar. All of them had the signature of each model.

Hussy stared at the picture of Saskia, trying to discern something from it. He felt the writing and the signature was flat. A phony, but still the one Rick had left there for so long after the page had started to yellow. In one box it said: "Today."

Hussy went through the other months. Nothing on the little sections for each day. He had assumed Acton was a moronic racist, but this woman was clearly and wonderfully Middle Eastern.

Hmm... Acton's desk was cluttered with papers – old cases and a couple of ongoing ones. There was nothing Hussy didn't know about.

He looked at the paperwork in front of him and the words danced. When he shut his eyes and concentrated fully, sentences would flow again, his brain slowly unscrambling. A document would reform into a few sentences, with all the lies removed.

He never understood why his mind worked that way, and he never questioned it.

The drawers had some more of that. Some pencils too, leaky pens, a half-empty Kleenex box, some paper clips. Under the desk and chairs was some dust and antique chewing gum.

He pulled the drawers out. Stuck with a little bit of tape to the bottom drawer was a key.

Hussy peeled it off and tried it in Acton's filing cabinet. Yes, a fit... and inside, under some Playboys, were ten photos.

He had seen one before: a blurred picture of Lenny Smith, another goon cop. He was very tall and he had a big gap between his teeth. He was handing some money to a suspicious guy with shades on. The man had a red arrow pointing to him with "DEALER" written at the end, a note for Acton's addled mind.

Everyone knew the police were corrupt. Protection,

payoffs, solicitation. They expanded so much energy covering their own backs, the rest of their brains struggled to cope. That led to long-winded speeches, coughing, and a general malaise.

James Bowles was now the Head of the local C.I.D. Hussy had gone to college with him and had a festering hatred of him. He was the pretty boy who always got the girl. He was the phony who passed his exams by spouting inanities.

There was a question in their Philosophy exam:

"What is courage?"

Hussy launched into an answer at ten-speed.

Bowles had written: "This is," and walked out of the exam hall. His teacher proudly showed his "A" grade to anyone she could on Results' Day. Hussy's "A" was an irrelevance, much like his life.

Bowles was ideal for "The Force," which he always called his job in a desperate attempt to impress power.

Hussy was aware he used to smoke weed a great deal. So, when he became a cop, Bowles knew where the students went to smoke. He would go there in an unmarked car. He'd commandeer the weed, make a show of throwing some of it in the river and then keep the rest of it for himself.

Lenny Smith was his partner in crime and, therefore, untouchable.

These futile thoughts rushed and Hussy started to doze. There was a throbbing behind his left ear, matching the rhythm of his heart.

Hussy stared at the photo of Lenny Smith resting on top of the pile.

And then Lenny – suddenly animated – started talking to him: "You mean you never did nothing wrong?" His hand came out in 3D and shook a finger at Hussy.

"Not like that," Hussy said.

"Yeah, yeah, yeah…" Lenny's head popped out and his nose touched Hussy's. Little gusts of garlic breath puffed out between the gap in his teeth.

Hussy slapped himself across the face and woke up.

He don't know why Rick bothered. Truth was for losers like Hussy. All that would happen was some cops would lie low then emerge like a whack-a-mole a year or so later.

He pushed back the brim of his hat, got up and walked over to the window and prised apart the blinds. The light was filtered by encrusted dirt.

Hussy strained at the catch. It eventually came open and he inhaled the thin but cool air.

Down below, thousand of ants went about their business in a patternless riot. The wind slid calmly around Hussy as he stared down at a world he struggled so hard to understand.

Something caught his eye. He shut the window, went back and turned off all the lights.

There was a long black car far below, and he sensed it was for him. A paranoid thought, but it looked like a hearse. It felt real enough as he looked at the name cast on the floor in dim shadows from the light of the office: "Rick Acton and Steve Hussy."

Ah well... he was ready. He just needed to scrape off Acton's name and let someone else take care of his.

20

"Any luck?" Fran said, looking up from her desk.

"Nope. Nothing."

She pursed her lips: "I'm sure something will pop up."

"We'll see."

"I called the police. The desk guy said you shouldn't touch Rick's office 'cause they might come and search it later."

"Fat chance."

"I knew you'd say that. Anyway, he sent the ballistics' details to me," she smiled her wide-eyed smile. "I printed them off. Want a peek?"

"Uh-huh." Fran passed him the sheet of A4. He turned it over. There was nothing on the back. "In-depth."

It said: "Shot in the head. Close range. Small handgun."

Hussy asked: "Anything else?"

"Not really. He said that forensics were having a tough because of all of the rain."

"Hmm."

"They said that he was shot at about 1 a.m., and then he

said: 'that I shouldn't worry and that they'll sort everything out for me.'"

Fran smiled and Hussy laughed a bit: "How sweet."

"Steve," she said, now serious. "What'll we do now?"

"I don't know."

"What about the other cases?"

"Put them on hold. Until we find who killed Jerk."

"Rick."

"I said that. We're hardly going to disappoint hundreds of clients." Business was slow. "Stall Lanny Curtis, ok? We can do the sting later."

"Sure. What are you going to do?"

"I'm going to watch some films and wait 'til tonight."

"Well, hey, don't work too hard!" she told him as he walked away, deliberately over-loud.

"Indeed!" He went into his bedroom and locked the door.

Hussy sat down and thought again, looking at the movie posters that surrounded him. He started to investigate his own life.

The fact Hussy wasn't with a woman indicated some severe mental illness to other people. He wished he had some name for it.

He was neither pan, bi, gay, or trans. He was merely ugly and straight. He was therefore someone who did not deserve a partner. But, like the Invisible Man with bandages wrapped around his face, or the Elephant Man with his cruel deformities, the ugliness had made him feel stronger.

He learned not to care about what came out of other people's mouths. All he could do was control what came out of his own... and most his words were a poke at the bland, selfish jibes that the normal foisted onto anyone different.

Then he fell asleep, his tongue lolling out of his mouth as he slumped on his sofa.

Hussy had the recurring dream again. The happy one. He was a child, four years old. At kindergarten he was building a fort around himself. He was very happy, and whenever he woke up the memory would cause Hussy to smile.

21

Hussy had soon found out that most P.I. jobs were boring. Summons, injunctions, digging up divorce grounds, checking up on partners, locating people and stolen pets. The work was sometimes for civilians but often for businesses searching for debtors. People could do it themselves if they had the brains...

Reality was already becoming disseminated and reformed. With more information came an urgent need to lie most effectively. The mass populous was still getting used to the Internet, a hive of information if you knew what you were doing.

The key was to watch and research. A VPN to protect any infiltration was the first step. Then he could slip in and out of the ether with yet more unseen, ghostly footprints.

Hussy searched through records, online accounts, and emailed people. He'd stare at a screen so much his eyes would burn.

Sometimes he would have to enter the underbelly of society and swim in the bile. Idiots, losers, narcissists, sloths. The jealous and the foolish. He blended in perfectly to the world, and that was added to by Acton's zoom lens and spyholes that Acton drilled himself with his dirty little drill.

Now and then Hussy would do something useful. Thieves, rapists, drug-dealers. But this – Acton being killed with a gun – was as rare as hen's teeth. Why didn't the killer just stab him?

Hussy's mind drifted through all this mess of thoughts as he watched *Night of the Hunter* for the umpteenth time.

He day-nightmared, consciously this time, about last March. It rumbled around his mind and his stomach ever since that night, but some part of him refused to make the connection with Acton's death because they had been so very careful.

Hussy was staking out a hotel with Acton. A guy's girl, Deanna, wanted to know where her man went to some nights. She had a good figure and a cute face that belied her taste for revenge.

They followed the man to a seedy bed and breakfast in a seedy area of Yarmouth.

The hotel had no name. The neon sign should have missed to O and the T to be exactly perfect. It had vacancies, and they expected some women-for-hire along pretty soon.

They saw one teenager – maybe 16 or 17 – go in and then come out shortly afterwards. Her hood was firmly over her head, but you could see her eyes and lips peeping out impassively.

"You think she's delivering something?" said Acton.

"Hmm," said Hussy, with no clue about what was actually going on.

"As long as she's over 18, every hole's a goal."

Acton almost smiled as Hussy coughed on his coffee: "WHAT?" If only he could break his own rule about swearing...

It was the first time he had been in Acton's car. Hussy was struggling to deal with the smell, even after cracking the window open and letting some cold rain speckle his face.

Rick smoked, didn't wash enough, and he'd clearly drank more of his ash-smelling whisky from the night before.

"Close the window," Acton said.

It was 4 a.m. and Hussy was watching shadows through a window. He was tired and irritable: "You reek of urine."

"Do I?" Acton finished his cigarette, opened the window and threw it out. That drew in more wind and rain. "Ah, get used it, boy. This job stinks pretty much all the time."

"Doesn't mean you have to."

The wind died down. The street quietly expected. The house were mostly boarded... ready to be reclaimed by the government and re-purposed. Hopefully for good reasons.

"Who the hell is that?" Acton said, and they immediately

slid down out of sight.

It was a black man, moving with elegance through the door. He had a leather case in his right hand.

"Maybe lover-boy plays for the other team?" Rick peered up through his camera.

"What's he doing?" Hussy tried to focus, yet saw nothing but blurs.

"He's closed the curtains and he's still messing around with his case." Acton cursed, then: "I can't see. We're too low."

Hussy drank his vodka – hidden in a little water bottle – and withheld the sighs that filled his being.

"'pect he's getting ready for action," Rick choked out a phlegmy cough. "He's heard a knock. He's going to answer it… I can barely see anything…"

The rain pounded on the roof of the car. Three shots rang out over the rain. More rain. One more shot. Then the rain pounded some more. Nothing in the street changed. No-one turned their lights on. No-one came out. No cops' sirens.

Hussy stared at Acton.

Acton said "Get down," and they lowered in their seats.

He whispered: "Wait…" Hussy knew Acton had to find out what was going on, for whatever twisted reason: "Now, let's go." Hussy and Acton put on their leather gloves and opened the doors of their car. The black man was walking fast and peering all around. He heard them, turned and ran up the alley by the side of the hotel. Acton cursed as they set off in pursuit.

Hussy was athletic but he was built for endurance not speed. His long legs and skinny body couldn't move any quicker. As Acton quickly panted to a near stop, the black man lengthened the gap between himself and Hussy, through three back streets into a dead-end.

The driving rain made a mist. The alley was empty. For twenty seconds, Hussy strained to look around. Nothing but a skip and the sky throwing down dark rain.

"Jesus. The nig-nog has disappeared." Rick said blandly as he caught up. He puffed and looked around, and Hussy simmered with rage at him.

There was clang from above. The emergency ladder to the roof. The man was now quickly climbing it. Hussy went up the steel steps and Acton followed, whining.

"Nig-nog's too fast for us."

Hussy clenched the rungs as if they were Rick's throat.

They reached the roof. It was a maze of shadows and chimneys. The acrid smoke smelled better than Acton's car.

Hussy followed the sound of driving wet footsteps. Rick shuffled behind getting slower and louder. Hussy stopped when the footsteps ahead stopped. Acton caught up with him, and quietly moved forward. An empty rooftop with nothing but the sky and the rain.

Rick whispered: "Stupid nig-nog's hiding in the shadows. Damn that nig-"

Hussy swung his fist around and connected in the centre

of Acton's nose. Acton fell into a puddle and out of consciousness, dropping his gun as he did so. Hussy looked down at a pathetic human being.

Hussy picked up the gun and crept around the chimneys.

It was soaking wet and silent. Just him and the rain again.

A large hand jabbed down, knocking his gun away.

Hussy said, as impassive as ever: "Ow."

The man stepped out from behind a chimney then backed away. His right hand had a handgun. He held it sideways. A 16-wheeler passed, then there was only the sound of the man's breath on the wind. He looked young, twenty or so. Close black hair, handsome face with big brown eyes. He had a red gash under his left arm. His blue jeans were darkened by the rain and the blood. Steam rose from his skin.

"You ain't taking me, pig." His eyes were wide and scared.

"I'm not a cop," Hussy backed off.

"I don't care what you are," he said. "You ain't taking me in."

Hussy remembered trying to say something in the moment of being caught between life and what happened.

"Don't," was all he came up with.

The man shook his head. His eyes were sad. "Do you know what he did? DO YOU KNOW WHAT HE DID?"

He waved his gun and shook his head, then waved his gun some more. He fired off a shot, but it was metres away from Hussy's head.

Hussy backed away even further: "It's ok."

The man twitched at seeing a red light passing his eyes, then he followed the red dot that travelled to the centre of his chest.

He looked at Hussy. He opened his mouth. There was a little "pop" as his chest exploded. He staggered back and fell off the building, with the same frozen expression all the way.

Hussy rushed to the edge of the building and peered over. The man lay face up, his arms splayed out in a pool of red with his gun still clenched in his right hand. The puddles were red too, reflecting the neon.

Hussy pale blue eyes stared into the man's brown eyes. Still no noise from the street, no reaction, no traffic and no CCTV.

He heard footsteps shuffle towards him and then Acton was next to him, peering over the edge too. It was only the second time Hussy had seen a dead body.

"You owe me one," Acton said, "boy."

"He wouldn't have shot me."

"He would've."

They made their way from the edge and down the ladder and back towards the hotel at the other end of the street.

Rick felt his jaw. "Nice right," he said.

Hussy stayed silent.

The lobby was as clean as a cop. The desk-man was on the floor, rubbing his head. A little snowstorm fell on his shoulders as he pushed to lift himself to his feet. He nodded to

Acton, who nodded back.

A TV blared out a late-night movie.

"Room 6, I reckon," he said. He got up and stumbled over to his chair. He supped at a mug of coffee and his sweat trickled down in thin brown trails. A bad dye job and a dirty human being. Hussy could smell dung from a hundred yards.

Acton led the way up. 6 was open. They creaked in.

Deanna's guy was splayed over the bed. He was good-looking, built like a bull. A gun laid by his right hand, with white powder stuck on to his staring face, the bed and the floor. The pools of red collected the white.

Acton took his gloved hand and called the police.

A television in the corner showed *Looney Tunes*. They watched the cartoons for a few minutes, unwilling to touch anything. Then they went down the stairs again to the desk-guy who was sweating even more profusely.

Hussy said: "What happened?" and his fists flexed again.

"I don't know, I really don't," said the man with the increasing brown trails on his head, "I was asleep."

22

The pit in Hussy's stomach had grown over the six months after that night. The procedures of the case lumbered on. He knew he was trapped... how could he quit now? He drank more booze to further nullify himself and amplify his narcolepsy.

Newspapers were largely disinterested in the case. A few reports at first, then almost nothing until it went to trial.

Acton revelled in the brief pieces of attention he received. He knew, through the few friends like Marcus in "The Force," that he wouldn't be in any legal trouble: "That numpty on the desk knew the punk in the room was selling dope to kids."

Hussy scratched at the side of his ear and wished he could sleep: "How did he make money? Kids don't have money."

"Sexual favours."

Now Hussy kneaded his forehead.

"He raped one of them," Acton almost said it with antipathy, "and she was only sixteen. Turns out that nig-nog..."

"Don't."

Acton ploughed on, "...was the girl's BROTHER."

No, no, no.

"It's a rough business," Acton, again, almost smiled. Hussy definitely saw that hint of a smile and it sickened him. Acton said: "I saved your life."

"Ah," and Hussy shut his eyes again.

"And at least Deanna is single now."

Hussy's fists clenched in his pockets.

But, within a year, those things passed.

Life trudged along, unaffected by the horror that had preceded it. Hussy stored it away as another horrible dream.

23

Hussy's mind drifted back to his room next to the office.

He heard a scuffling at the window, clicked the catch on the window and pulled it up.

Bogey jumped in, wet and grumpy. He gave a plaintive "meow."

Remorseless green eyes stared at Hussy. Bogey had perfected his "look." It could penetrate lead and it came in different versions: "I want food," "I want attention" and "Clean my litter tray." Hussy discerned Bogey wanted food this time.

He knew Bogey travelled around and had multiple food sources. He had a flap in the fire escape door but he liked scratching the window. It was the feline equivalent of nails on a blackboard.

Bogey would disappear for a few days and come back fatter. A perfect gold-digger with pale blonde fur and a black belly. A maine-coon crossed with another breed. A beautiful, fascinating mongrel.

Hussy said: "Hello, Bogey."

He looked up at Hussy then at the fridge door.

"Yeah, yeah, yeah..." He took out the chicken, and Bogey rubbed his sharp face against his hand. Then the cat leisurely ate the food.

Hussy watched him the whole time. Strange pale blue eyes tried to process something embedded deep in his brain.

Bogey finished, rubbed against his hand again, went in the basket next to Hussy's bed and fell asleep.

Hussy sat on the bed and continued to watch Bogey. His belly went up and down, then his whiskers started to twitch.

He had removed all the mirrors from the office and his room, but now he would sometimes clench his fists and look at them. He had oversized, strong hands. He looked at them, then he looked at Bogey.

Bogey had simple pleasures but he was happy. He ate and slept and got stroked and got very excited over yarn. If man's greatest pleasure was playing with a bit of string maybe the world would be a better place...

Those whiskers kept on twitching, then his eyes shot open. "HEY. What're you staring at?" Bogey said. "Why'd you let Acton shoot the kid that night?"

"I couldn't do..."

"Why didn't you hear him?"

"I..."

"You're not Dr. Doolittle. And you're the pussy, not me."

Hussy took his big right hand and slapped himself across the face. He opened his eyes, and saw Bogey was still asleep.

He went back into his office, head down.

"WHATCHU DOIN'?" Fran almost shouted.

The noise startled him and he veered away from it.

"It's only me." She stared at him, those honey coloured eyes reading his brain: "Have you taken your meds today?"

"Yeah."

"OK." She was standing against the desk. Her lipstick was pink. She had a long-sleeved sweater in dark red. Her skirt was dark brown, suede, short. Three inch club-heeled black leather knee boots. Six inches of thigh looked as close to heaven as Hussy would ever get.

"AHEM." Fran had her tongue against her cheek.

He said: "Nice boots," and his face flushed.

"Thanks. Not too slutty?"

"Nah..."

"I hated those suits I had to wear, y'know," and she beamed.

Hussy laughed at that: "Rick didn't."

"Don't remind me."

"Of Kleenex?"

"URGH!"

"Ah, he was what he was..."

Fran shrugged: "I've never seen your room, y'know."

"You're not missing much."

"You got anything else for me to do, Mr. Workaholic?"

Thoughts tangled in Hussy's head: "You want to watch a movie until I think of something?"

"I could get jump cables for your noodle."

"Funny."

"I know."

"So... Movie?"

"Yeah."

Hussy frowned: "We should do *something*." His mind was filled with thoughts he struggled to express: "Any ideas?"

"You're the one with the license."

"I think I have a plan."

"Wanna tell me what it is?"

"Maybe later."

Fran asked: "What're we going to watch?"

"The greatest film ever."

"*The Room*?"

Hussy pulled the brim of his hat down: "*CASABLANCA!*"

"Oh."

"It's really good."

"As long as it's not *The Omega Man* again..."

"I thought you'd like it."

She smiled: "I fell asleep."

Leering was so much easier when she was asleep... "Even with your taste you'll like this." But he couldn't bring himself to touch her. His moral code was stultifying.

"Time for some STRONG coffee then," Fran pouted.

"I try to be nice in this world and..."

Fran smiled and left.

He slid out the small bottle of vodka from his pocket, chugged it down without a wince, got the DVD out of its cardboard case, shoved it in, thought a bit, then shouted: "LOOK. EVEN I CAN'T FALL ASLEEP THROUGH THIS ONE."

Fran laughed a non-mocking laugh and shouted back: "WANNA BET?"

24

Hussy said: "I'm thirsty" to the bartender.

The bar was still unchanged, empty except for them. It was a retreat from the gastropubs and their foul smells, and the popular pubs with their endless, meaningless chatter.

Dry mouth over women is nothing new, I'm afraid.

"Hmm." If he sought anything, it was silence. He wanted to lose himself in his mind.

You've never talked this much either, have you?

Peter knew his stuff.

Hussy drank the new glass of red wine, then: "No."

Care for some water?

"Thanks." He put it in the glass he'd been polishing. It was cold and refreshing.

"Nice goatee, by the way."

I thought I'd give it a try.

He was maybe 50. White hair. Calm.

"Want to hear some more?"

Oh, yes. I do so enjoy a good story.

Hussy felt a weight of pressure. He had since he was a kid.

25

Fran came back in and put their coffee cups on the low table before them.

She tugged at her skirt after she sat down: "Ready?"

"Uh-huh," and he started the movie.

He watched closely throughout, but his roving eyes only caught some of *Casablanca*. Being around Fran's beauty still made Hussy feel less ugly. They sat in silence, and he enjoyed the sound of her breath. He was a lost cause...

"Well," Fran had stayed awake throughout, and turned away at the end. Either it had moved her or she looked at Hussy and her eyes had gone into trauma: "Why would that Else woman go out with your mate Hump-free anyway?"

"He's cool."

"As if that matters!"

Hussy stuck his white-flecked tongue out: "Don't make me set mini-Bogey on you."

She pursed her lips to one side: "Shut up. Mini-Bogey loves me. He purrs like crazy..." She gave him a little punch on the shoulder. "I did love the crazy guy."

"Peter Lorre?"

"I like his eyes."

"I like his voice."

Fran paused, then, "Steve?"

"Ah?"

"What are we gonna do?"

"We're gonna do the best we can."

"You old softy." And the "we" smiled together. "Want some coffee, boss?"

"It's gone five," he said. "Your working day is done."

She grinned, put on her short puffy jacket that stopped at the waist and gripped there.

"Fran," Hussy said. "What do you do for fun?"

She stared at him, making him turn away. That made her smile: "I play the saxophone."

He snapped back and looked at her in the eyes again with something like shock: "The saxophone?"

"Yes," she said it all with a casual smile – a question she must have answered a thousand times before: "and don't look at me like that."

Hussy blushed: "Are you good?"

"It's hard to explain. I can play anything but I can't get the raspiness."

"Would you play for me?"

That made her beam: "No!"

Hussy's mind tried to do its usual computations.

Fran shoved his arm... "Stop looking like that. More movies, ok?"

"Always."

"Bye."

"See ya."

He watched her leave, and he had a bizarre thought. Fran had a black coat on and he had a black suit on.

It was as close as they'd get to mourning Acton's death.

Hussy unlocked the door to his bedroom and walked into his cave.

26

Hussy pulled a bottle of Pinot Noir from a small cupboard and poured it into a large glass. He never drank wine or beer during the day. He also never drank in bars with more than two other people.

Hussy took his dinner out of his small freezer, sliced the top open and placed it in the microwave and set the thing going.

PING.

He took the first mouthful and winced, then kept eating by washing it down with the wine. He chewed and stared at the wall, the speed and his meds fuelling his overactive brain.

He thought about Fran. She was right. Real life isn't like the movies. Only in Hollywood could a good guy who looked like Bogey end up with so many beautiful women falling at his feet.

The walls of his bedroom were stacked floor to ceiling with books on one side, and DVDs covering the three remaining walls. The only breaks were the door into his office, the door into his shower room, and one poster on each wall.

Narcoleptic

He had carefully searched for each of the posters. *In A Lonely Place, The Big Combo, Nightmare Alley,* and his favourite – *Blast of Silence*. After searching on eBay for months, eventually an original was listed in the USA. He stayed awake, helped by speed, until 5 in the morning to snipe the final bid. No-one else bid, and that in itself was part of the joy of loving the film.

Like Frankie Bono, Hussy knew he would not get the girl. He knew he would be betrayed – by himself or someone else. And he deeply felt he'd also end up dead in a cold, winter river.

He drank his wine and stared through another waking day-nightmare. They were so different from the elaborate, phony, plot-driven dreams.

Aged 18, Hussy been considered odd and isolated, even while the narcolepsy was milder. Acne-ridden pale skin, overly large nostrils and always those strange blue eyes.

For two years he had been lusting over a girl in his English Literature class: Rachael Recci.

Rachael had a mid-brown hair, long legs, the good kind of top-heaviness, and brown catlike eyes. She came across as sweet and she was smart too... not easy given the surroundings.

The college was a dump. The most backward and run-down of places, lazily converted from a hellhole of a Victorian school. Some students foraged for knowledge, but the rest foraged for relationships, adding to the town's proud history of having the highest teenage pregnancy rate in England.

Rachael got a lot of attention. Maybe she could fix their

Norfolk, hillbilly gene-pool? She was the hope of most students.

Hussy had caught a break a few months before. The kindly English Literature teacher had stuck them together on a coursework project on *Julius Caesar*. They were the two students with the highest grades. She had hoped to make them soar, but also hoped to make Hussy talk. He had so many words on paper, but so few came out of his mouth.

Rachael had smiled: "Let's smash this."

And he had said: "Hmm."

Hussy came up with the concept of turning *Julius Caesar* into a film noir. 5000 words transferred into a short story.

They rewrote the characters. Caesar as the mob boss, Brutus and Cassius as made-men wanting to take over the Mafia, Portia turned into a gangster's moll... and on and on.

It was easy and fun.

Rachael had laughed a lot over the few weeks. It was only ten hours, but they were filled with laughter.

The memories slid into Hussy's head like an icepick. Results Day. She was glistening away with a group of friends, female and male, all with pieces of paper in their hand. Many were laughing, released from the pressure of exams.

She smiled at Hussy: "I got an A in Literature!"

"That's great," he said, "I did too!"

Hussy stood awkwardly, unsure whether to hug her or whether she wanted to hug him.

He pulled up his tall body: "Can I ask you something?"

"Sure."

He said it quietly: "Wanna go out with me sometime?"

Rachael's mouth gaped open and her eyes widened. Then they narrowed and the corners of her mouth lifted a little. Then her eyes closed, she pursed her lips as if she was in pain. Then she convulsed and started to laugh. She gasped for breaths.

Hussy stood, mute, as the rest of the group turned.

"I'm sorry," Rachael blurted in the gasps. "It's just..."

Hussy tried to wake from the nightmarish memory, but his eyelids wouldn't move. He was frozen, trapped like amber.

Rachael's lips began to stretch. Her hair began to writhe. Her face became a large mouth with snakes instead of a tongue.

He said: "It's cool. Just a little joke. Haha."

People started to gather around. Their eyes grew bigger, merging into cyclops. Eventually they all had a big eye for a head. The black irises swelled, then opened and closed like mouths.

They all started to sing like Screaming Jay Hawkins: "I put a spell on you... 'cause your mine..."

The eye-heads did a formation dance together.

"Stop the things you do..."

Hussy started to dance too, involuntarily. Strange movements.

"HAHA... WATCH OUT! I AIN'T LYING. YEAAAAAAH."

The fork clattered against Hussy's plate. It pinged off a piece of soya and landed on the floor.

His eyes bolted awake and then he slumped back.

He looked at Bogey. He was still asleep. If only he could be a cat? He was not built to be a human being...

Hussy dutifully washed, urinated, brushed his teeth, pulled out the futon, and waited to see whether the night would bring a better storyline than the truth.

Something like a plan continued to formulate in the further strange images he dreamed that night.

In the morning, he wrote in his neat, even handwriting:

Get Jen out of Rick's flat.

Search Rick's flat.

Go around the seedy strip clubs.

See who kills me first.

He scrubbed out the last line and replaced it with:

Carry a gun and wear the stab-proof vest.

Become a hero to Francesca.

He smiled ruefully, took his morning meds and washed them down with six shots of vodka in the water. He held up the bottle to the light, then tucked it away again.

27

"You got anything for me to do, then, bosssssss?" Fran took her jacket off slowly and shuddered. Her cheeks were flushed.

Hussy said: "Yep."

"Oooh."

"Can you find Rick's address, please?"

"Don't you know it already?"

"No, *you* know it. I've never been there. You do the wage slips."

"Alright."

Hussy breathed in and said: "That's the easy part..."

She cocked her head.

Hussy quickly said: "Can you ring Jen and make sure to take her somewhere for a couple of hours."

Fran's eyes widened: "But she's a nightmare!"

"I know," Hussy said, "just console her."

"CONSOLE HER? Does she even feel emotions?"

"Get her drunk. I'll pay for it. Just keep her away."

"A day in hell with Little Miss Blobby," but there was something like a smile coming over Fran's face. "Don't be surprised if your coffee tastes funny from now on..."

"It already does," then he smiled too. "I'll be in my office."

"Alright..."

He went into his room and got some water. He then diluted it with yet more vodka, and took some more meds and amphetamine with it.

He went back into his office, locked the bedroom door, and rested with his face on the desk.

Fran knocked and he bolted upright. She propped herself against the door arch.

He said: "That was quick."

"It's 12 Roman Road."

"I've heard of it. It's near."

"And Jen isn't even there," Fran said. "She said she can't face it."

"Is she ok to meet up?"

"We're going to 'drown our sorrows' – as The Blob told me – in The Troll Cart."

"Apt."

Fran gritted her teeth: "My sorrow will be listening to her damn mouth."

"Ah, be nice."

"Nope!" Fran's eyes followed Hussy as he plonked on a standard day coat, gloves, and an inconspicuous, unbranded baseball cap. "What're you gonna do?"

"Search it."

"Won't the police be there?"

"Doubtful. They're not trying."

"How do you know?"

"They haven't questioned me yet," Hussy said. "And I'm their prime suspect."

"WHAT?"

"I'm the only one with a motive. That I know of, anyway."

"Which is?"

"This place. I own it now. It's not much, but it's a motive."

"Steve..." she said with care, "have you got an alibi?"

"Nah. Asleep. For a change."

"Aren't you worried?"

"Nah."

"Why?"

"The evidence isn't there for anyone, and the killer used a different gun from mine. The hole was too big."

"Well, ok... How're you going to get in?"

He held up Acton's spare apartment key, taken from Acton's office drawer.

Fran smiled, stepped back and Hussy made for the exit.

"Steve," she said, "what happens if you get killed?"

He turned and lifted his arms: "You get all this!"

She stuck her little pink tongue between her brown lips, went PHWAP with it, and said: "Then don't get killed, ok?"

"Eh..." He went cross-eyed as he said: "Make sure to lock up, ok?"

The door eased back shut behind him. Hussy rested his back against it and smiled broadly.

28

The doors of the Hussy's building were open. Masses of people were going to and from the shopping centre. They jostled and droned over the hum of the traffic. A stick insect with parcels swore at him as he tried to glide through the swarm of people.

Every face had a blank look... endless ants who had just spent money or were determined they were going to.

Hussy walked towards The Troll Cart and flagged for a taxi. They were lined up outside the pub, capturing the drunk and the desperate... and charging accordingly.

Hussy looked at the driver's ID card... he was called McGowan. He had a knowing smile, tuned the radio to Bach, said "Hey Buddy" and nothing else. It was a perfect, dignified trip.

Roman Road had beat-up cars and beat-up houses. Number 12 was another Lego piece stuck in a landfill site. Six windows, each with different decor.

He felt all of the windows watching him. Compound eyes of more insects. He'd be easy to pick off too, and he knew his reinforced vest would struggle with a bullet.

He asked to be dropped a half-mile from the building. He could walk forever, fuelled by booze and speed and his heart's desire to stay alive when his brain said the opposite.

The street was empty except for one. He was a tall man lazily smoking a cigarette opposite the building. Hussy glanced at him as he walked, but the tall man didn't look in his direction. The man took draws from his cigarette, sending out wisps of smoke as he stared sullenly at the ground.

Hussy paused for the briefest of moments, and the man reached inside his pocket. A gun? No, no... too hard to get hold of. Hussy feared death less than constipation anyway.

The man pulled out a mobile phone instead. These

burgeoning toys were a cancerous boil on the anus of mankind. They sucked the life out everything.

What was so exciting on a Nokia screen? What was so much better than in a page, or in a wide-screen cinema, or in the shifting panorama of life itself?

The man didn't raise his head, and Hussy focussed his attention at the pink clouds trying to force their way through the mist.

When he turned, the tall man was loping away, still checking his phone. What was happening to humanity?

Hussy used the first key to get inside.

The carpet was brown and thin, and some concrete showed through. It was sticky, and Hussy tried not to think why. The wallpaper was beige, swirly and equally thin.

There was a corridor and 3 doors on the ground floor. A, B and C. Hussy was used to filth – he'd grown up in it – but he didn't understand why Acton would live here. Where had his money gone over so many years?

He hated the sound of his feet creaking on the stairs and the tackiness of whatever filth was on them. This was stupid…

The second floor was like the first, with the bonus of a guy bursting out of a room. Hussy had finally found someone.

He tried to swagger towards the man, trying to channel his inner Robert Mitchum.

Hussy said, "Who the hell are you?" Then he instantly regretted not being more polite.

29

Hussy eyes stung and he squinted against the fluorescent lights in the bar.

So?

Hussy had been used to the dark for so long, the light represented something more painful than the shadows.

You look like you could do with something.

"Maybe..." Hussy shrugged: "... Peter... Nice name tag."

Not my idea, might I add. Red wine?

"Yeah." Peter poured. Hussy drank half of it in one gulp.

Do you need some time to think?

"Nah. It's all in there. Floating around. Everything."

Useful.

"You'd think so and, yeah, for quizzes and exams it is."

But?

"But it's messed me up. I've had more bad than good and I remember it all. The horror floats up like a corpse."

History helps you learn.

"Maybe for some." Hussy sighed. "But nothing happens the same again." Now he shut his eyes and kneaded them, trying to force whatever truth he had out of himself. "You do something that works once, and it doesn't again. You change something that should've stayed the same. You stay the same when you should've changed. It's like one endless trick question."

Maybe.

"Maybe I just couldn't work out the answers."

He finished the wine.

Better?

"Yeah. One answer found. Again."

More?

"Always."

Keep going...

30

The man turned and looked at Hussy. He was even bigger than Hussy. 6'6" and built like a wrestler. All muscles and gut.

He had a big forehead and curly blond hair on top. Two big eyebrows with cheap sunglasses. An even face with bull nostrils snorting down onto the smaller Hussy.

Hussy kept going forward, keeping his eyes fixed on the goon. The floorboards creaked some more, and Room F's door clicked open a tiny amount.

The goon looked at the keys in his hand. Then he pulled in his lips and stuck out his chin. He looked at Hussy. He put the keys in his right pocket without looking down. He took off his black leather gloves and stuck them in the same pocket. LOVE and HATE were – stupidly – on his knuckles. He should have opted for LEFT and RITE.

The goon breathed in. Light-fittings tinkled. Pictures on

the wall were drawn towards him. He breathed out and charged.

Hussy said: "Oh," and side-stepped gracefully to the right.

For a split second Hussy waited for ol' rightie to miss him so he could turn and sucker-punch the goon in the temple.

SMACK.

The goon's left hand rammed into Hussy's right eye, making a sound like a twenty-storey jumper meeting concrete. He reeled back against the wall, and rubbed the eye to check it was still there.

Hussy kicked out with his right foot and connected with the goon's knee.

The man swore but kept charging past Hussy. The goon reeled down the stairs, out of sync but oh-so loud.

"HEY!" Hussy shouted, words reverberating in his brain.

He watched the man with his one good eye and fumbled in his pocket for his gun. He just found his hip flask instead.

The goon made it out of the door, his feet loudly slapping all the way.

Hussy's brain ran but his legs didn't. They thought he should have a little rest on the floor, so he did. Watery blood seeped down from his eye.

Hussy took a long swig from the flask.

Why couldn't the guy have punched him into his vest instead? He took another swig and smiled at the creak of a door opening further. Ah, just kill him now... He was ready.

31

"Are you OK?" said a tiny voice.

Hussy looked at the dark slit where Room F's door was ajar. An eye reflected the light.

He said: "I've had better days."

"Are you a policeman?" A woman's voice, croaky but kind.

"No, never that." Then he said: "I'm a private detective."

"Do you know Mr. Acton?"

"I was Rick's partner."

"Really?"

Hussy detected the undertones of saying that: "Detective partner, that is."

"Small world isn't it?"

Hussy tucked away his hip flask, then drew out his license and showed it to the woman.

"That's me," he said, pointing to the young ugly dude.

She opened the door a little more. The chain was on and it rattled. She was 70 or 80 with grey skin, drawn back grey hair, gold rimmed glasses and a white woolly cardigan. He glimpsed a poker in her right hand, but he couldn't see the left...

"Is Mr. Acton in trouble?" she said.

"Yes. He is."

"Wait there, please." She shut the door.

20 seconds passed.

The chain rattled again, the door creeped open and she

hobbled out in slo-mo. She had a metal cane in one hand and she was leaning on it heavily.

"Poor thing," she said, looking down at Hussy.

"Hmm."

"You'd better come in and tell me all about it." The left side of her face was frozen, but her voice was clear.

She offered her shaking right hand to help him up. He pushed himself up and made it through the door.

The wall of heat hit him. The air was paper thin and stank of pot-pourri.

"Take a seat, please, Mr..."

"Hussy."

"Mr. Hussy." Her little laugh tinkled: "Such a funny name."

Hussy smiled: "I get that a lot."

Then she smiled too: "I'll get you some tea and something for that poorly eye of yours."

"Thanks."

She lurched off into the kitchen.

The living room was large... twice the size of his office. There was the usual stuff crammed in there. A china unicorn, a mass of gold framed photos, Victorian paintings, a chicken made from dried flowers, pots with plants, pots without plants, brass pans, little figurines, plates, gilt angels. The brass poker now rested against the fireplace, where there was a log fire like a second sun blazing away.

Hussy made it to the flowery sofa without falling over

anything. He slid off his trenchcoat, but the sweat still dribbled down his face.

He shut his good eye, but opened it with a start when he heard the lady shuffling over.

"Here you are Mr. Hussy." She gave him a bag of frozen peas. He held it against his forehead and his bad eye.

"Thank you. Mrs.?"

"Ms," which she pronounced Mzzzz, "Maggie Pearson." She stared at his face. "He was a big nasty chap, wasn't he?"

He nodded, and he felt like a little kid.

"I'll get you some tea. That should help sort things out..."

32

Hussy sat there and felt the cold water drip down. Some infomercial came on the TV sitting inside a pine unit in the corner of the room.

He couldn't see a remote and he couldn't face moving to change the channel. The heat swelled again, and he felt he was stuck in hell.

A man almost jumped onto the screen.

"HI! I'm Mike Hunt!" He had blond nylon hair, glow-in-the-dark teeth and a freshly squeezed tan. The crew clapped off camera. The floor manager gave the obligatory whoop.

"And I'm going to tell about the new deluxe SUPER-

GRABBER." Hussy suspected he had snorted coke or drank far too much coffee. "Its new deluxe articulated grab-o-tron will pick up, lift and manipulate ANYTHING. That's right, everybody, ANYTHING."

"Elephants?" Hussy whispered.

Hunt waved the thing around: "C'mon... try the new deluxe Super Grabber, Tara!"

The host of the show wandered on screen with a big, phony grin. She was very pretty, with blazing curly red hair, but there was the deadness to her eyes that infect TV presenters. It was something beyond trying to read from the autocue... it was an interior death of the soul.

"Hello, you."

"Hey!"

"C'mon... you must be able to pick up ANYTHING."

She mock-winced and had the acting skills of a gherkin. "I'm always dropping papers and photos and stuff like that." She stretched out her back, pushing her breasts forward. "And my back isn't getting any younger." Some mutual laughs.

"Well, it just so happens we have a little test... a paper caught between two loose floorboards."

She took the Super-Grabber and expertly pulled the paper out.

"WOW!" they said in unison.

The red studio lights blazed away. The fire blazed away and Hussy's shirt was soaked with sweat and his head lolled forward.

The green stems on the sofa began to grow. They wrapped around his body and neck and sprouted large purple flowers. Some were roses, and the thorns started to cut in. Some looked like lilies, and they smelt of death. The flowers grew mouths. Some licked at the water dribbling from Hussy's forehead and slack mouth.

The walls started to pulse in time with the heartbeat pounding in Hussy's eye and head. The china unicorn walked towards him and cocked its head to one side. The dried-flower chicken danced and sang: "I feel like chicken tonight."

People in photos came to life. Some gave a cheery wave, some just smiled. Some of the smiling ones' lips moved as if they were saying something.

Hussy started to choke as the vines bound him to the sofa. The flowers were whispering something. He strained to hear, but the vines and thorns tightened around him.

Blood trickled from Hussy's neck, but all he did was smile as his one open eye accepted death.

33

The illusion was shattered with the sound of something rattling. Ms. Pearson shuffled up behind Hussy, and his head instinctively lurched upright.

The photos, the chicken, the unicorn and the walls went to sleep immediately.

"It must be time for my show soon," she said. She put a tray on the table. It had a teapot and two cups and some biscuits on it. "Now, where is my gizmo?"

Hussy watched her closely as she searched around. He desperately tried to stay awake.

Ms. Pearson drew out the remote from underneath the cushion of the armchair: "I like Quincy... He's so nice and he's got lovely hair."

There was nothing in her face to give her away. But why would she be in this neighbourhood?

"Jimmy and I used to watch it all the time."

Hussy asked: "Your husband?"

"Yes," she said. "He was a lovely man. He's over there on the mantelpiece." Her hand shook as she pointed.

He had been smiling at Hussy earlier. He was in a Royal Navy uniform. Now he looked composed, long faced and sad.

Pearson was smiling.

"You were looking at the photo next to him as well weren't you?"

"Hmm."

"That's my daughter. That's my Priscilla."

She looked like a cross between the Pilsbury Dough-Boy and a tub of lemon curd. The rest of the family were lined up. The boys were also weighty and they smiled big honest smiles.

"She seems like a nice lady."

"Taken, I'm afraid," she said as the opening credits of *Quincy M.D.* rolled. The poor medical trainee passed out yet again as Quincy drew out his pathologist's saw.

Hussy's swollen eye started to ease open. The white of his eye had turned red, but he still looked intently. "Do you mind if I open the door?" he asked. "In case someone comes along."

"Don't worry," she said. "Those floorboards creak ever so loud." Something like anger passed over her face. "You can hear everyone coming and going because they won't fix them…"

She poured the tea, and Hussy waited for her to drink first. She did and then he tried it. It was Earl Grey. The peas thawed as Quincy moaned at Asten for a while.

More adverts during which Pearson turned her attention to Hussy. Her left eye finally blinked. The other followed a few seconds later.

"Now what seems the problem with Mr. Acton?"

"He's dead."

She looked stunned: "He seemed like such a nice man…"

Hussy withheld a laugh at that: "Did you see him much?"

"I can't say I did, I'm afraid." Pearson didn't sound phony, it just seemed like she wanted to talk: "He always waved up at the window if I happened to be looking out. I would hear him come and go."

"How about last night?"

She supped at her cold tea: "It must have been 11 when

he left. *M.A.S.H.* was starting and I couldn't hear it because of those silly floorboards. They STILL won't fix them, you know?"

"Yes." Hussy was beading with more sweat.

"Did he have an accident, Mr. Hussy?"

"He got shot."

"Oh, dear." Her face was now fixed and inscrutable: "Why would anyone want to do that to Mr. Acton?"

"I was going to ask you that."

"I don't know if I can be much help, Mr. Hussy."

He prodded at his bad eye. It had sealed shut again, but he knew he would heal quickly. He liked to think of that as nature's ironic desire to maintain his ugly mug.

"That looks painful." She was too nice, but that was hard to quantify. "Can I get you some Co-Codamol?"

What was she? A crack dealer? A mob informant? A trained sniper with her cane that was obviously a gun?

"No, no, no." The sweat was now pouring from Hussy. He felt dizzy. "Really. I'm good. I'd better get going."

"Oh, well, you might as well finish your tea."

She reached for the cane and moved it closer to her.

He took a gulp of stone cold tea.

"Mr. Acton did have a lot of ladyfriends come round, if that's any help. Pretty young things with high heels. If I looked like that I'd flaunt it too!" She gave a wry smile and firmed her grip on the cane.

"Has Rick been around much recently?"

"Oh, yes. He's been coming and going a lot. I expect he was on holidays from work."

In the background, Quincy had already shouted "travesty of justice" at three different people. He had also brushed aside an attractive woman half his age to concentrate on his job. Now he was exposing "the truth."

"Did you see him with anyone recently?"

"No... I only hear those floorboards making that dreadful noise. I'm so sorry I can't help you more." He didn't know what to discern from her open face. "There was just that man last night, those heavy feet," she said. "I've never heard anything like it!"

Hussy cocked his head to the side: "I better have a look in Rick's apartment."

"Here, let me show you out..." She reached for the cane and closed her grip around it.

"NO, no... Mzzzzz Pearson."

"Well, thank you. It's was lovely to have a chat with you. If you would like to talk to me again, you know where I am."

"Yeah." He made it to the door unscathed: "Thanks."

"Please pass on my condolences to Mr. Acton's family."

"I will." He opened the door and gusts of cold air hit him. He drew in three deep breaths.

He heard: "Goodbye, Mr. Hussy" as he eased the door closed, and wanted for the Yale lock to click.

Hussy leaned against the door and listened. All he heard was Quincy having a beer with his cronies. Nothing more, nothing less.

He took a long swig of vodka from his hip-flask and within a minute the sweating and shaking started to ease.

He took out his gun with his right hand. The strain of his tight grip made his leather glove creak.

He went to Rick's door and listened carefully to that too.

Nothing, and there was no sign of forced entry. The goon had that key and he was far too heavy to shimmy up a drainpipe.

Hussy unlocked the door and it swung open smoothly.

34

He had expected Rick's apartment to be a pit.

It wasn't, but it did stink. Smoke, whiskey and sweat created an uncomfortable memory of Acton's stench. Plug-in room-fragrancers were artfully placed and they completed a smell reminiscent of a whorehouse.

The banalities of the room made him feel secure yet bored. Objects, clothes, furnishings.

The only mythological "clue" he was surprised by was Rick's taste in art. The paintings were silly nudes and portraits of handsome people, but Hussy's university had a decent art gallery and he recognised at least one of the works.

He was struck by a beautiful, lurid, near-naked woman by an artist who had hit semi-big over the next last years. It must have been worth £10,000 or so...

A couple of the other paintings seemed recognisable too... derivative versions of great Egon Schiele nudes. Hussy knew he had seen them before in the little gallery in Yarmouth's library. It was usually populated by art students who would – sometimes sadly – give up art as soon as they got a steady job. But back then they were being sold for... what, £1000, £2000? Why hadn't they been stolen? But what did that mean?

Hussy's problem was that the shell of people didn't interest him. That vague world of surface seemed like clues but he viewed them as quirks. A sheen of life, polished by people who needed to hide their deepest thoughts.

Hussy merely felt Acton was aiming for women with a taste for the finer things. In amongst the true "art," lifeless black and white photographs of beach locations featured in the centre of each free wall.

The bathroom and the kitchen were spotless. Even Rick's food was limited to noodles and cereal, and the fridge had a four pack of beer, a bottle of Grey Goose, and a coke mixer. Everything was so neatly arranged in there. Did he have a cleaner come in?

The living room and bedroom were in stark contrast. They had been thoroughly searched, and the Goon was not a tidy guy. If Hussy had disturbed him, then he had been nearing the end of whatever he was searching for. The soft furnishings had been sliced, the drawers had been emptied, and books had been rearranged into an abstract pattern on the floor.

Hussy seethed at this fictional world of "clues." A TV detective can find lint on the floor and work out the killer was 5'11" with brown hair. Nonsense...

Once you work out there aren't any of the obvious hints – lipstick on cigarettes, addresses on a matchbook, a signed note with "I'm gonna kill ya" – where do you go?

In Rick's room, one of the law books was open on page 666. Had it just fallen that way? Did the killer worship Satan?

Even the good clues were usually planted to throw you off and Hussy knew searching searched rooms would be a waste of time. He did it anyway.

What he found in drawers was ridiculous: Rick liked silk boxers, Marlboros and semi-secreted Playboys that opened straight to the articles.

There wasn't a wet patch on any floor and no smell of bleach. That told him that Acton hadn't been killed there, which shortened the list to a few million other places.

Hussy slumped on what was left of Rick's sofa. A spring pressed into his back. He felt his swollen eye again, then looked at the wall. It had a clock with a second hand that slid around smoothly so he couldn't count the seconds ticking away.

He had a bright idea. He got up and unhooked the clock and checked it over. Nothing but a battery. He sat down.

The room's smell made itself known again. That gave Hussy another idea. He yanked the fragrance plugs out of the walls. He ripped them apart... nothing except for little pieces of pink soap. He threw them in the bin and sat down again.

His leather gloves were soaked with the perfume. He tried to rub it off on his trousers... now they stank too. The smell overpowered him and, as ever, sleep came.

Hussy never felt rested. He twitched in his REM sleep, dreaming his dreams, never fully asleep and seldom fully awake.

This time he was a fragrant, pink origami pig. His left foreleg had a black spot just above the knee. His trotters were brown from the mud, and he was penned off by wooden fences. He had a good time pushing the slime between his two toes, but the dampness was slowly seeping through his paper legs.

Then another origami pig strutted over. It had a female voice: "You're not doing that right, idiot." She took a few steps back from the mud. It said: "You have to really get into it to cool down," and she took a running jump at it. She glided in, landed with a plop and started rolling in the mud. She grinned.

Her paper was soggy from the mud, but she was having a great time. She looked up: "You'll get sunburn otherwise."

"I..." was all he could manage to say.

The other pig's mouth opened far too wide and it screamed as a piercing alarm that vibrated through his body.

Hussy lurched awake.

His burner phone was ringing and vibrating.

"Get out of there NOW," Fran said.

"Is Jen coming?"

"STEVE. GET OUT," Fran huffed. "You've got ten minutes

tops, alright?"

"Alright."

Hussy went to the sink in the kitchen. He drank some cold water, popped in his meds and another dose of speed, then drank straight from the tap.

He wiped the inside of the sink with a tissue and pocketed it with his gloved hands.

He had a look out of the window. Through the yellow-brown he saw the black sky. The city stretched out. There were lights and ugly buildings.

The floorboards said "goodbye" in their own way and he stopped at Room F.

He felt bad about Ms. Pearson. She was a kind old lady. He found a twenty pound note and slipped it under the door. She could always buy bullets with it...

He made it to the stairs, heard the creak of her door opening, and looked back as the crack in the door asked: "Did you manage to find anything, Mr. Hussy?

"No luck."

"Never mind, my dear," Pearson said. "I hope something will turn up for you, Mr. Hussy."

"Thanks."

The door shut again, and the twenty pound note gently sneaked under the door.

35

It took a half-hour to get back to the Olympia. The traffic crawled and it was rush hour. The cab driver was courteous and then silent. It was McGowan again, and Hussy took him to be a beautiful Irishman at peace with the universe.

Hussy knew he could never find that peace, no matter how much whiskey he drank. Fear that he would miss Fran nagged at Hussy's mind, keeping him awake.

A crazy partner, a goon, an old lady. Each had the power to disturb him deeply. He wasn't cut out for this kind of work.

But Fran, Fran... The way she talked, the way she moved, that black-lipped and oh-so-broad smile, that sweater, those calves in those boots. In some ways, he knew he could die happy.

He walked up to his office, gently rubbing his bruised eye. It opened slightly as he looked at the now blurred writing on the agency's door. S. HUSSY P.I. would sum things up nicely. Or S. HUSSY and F. DAWN?

The light was still on, and the door was unlocked. He lowered his chin, and pulled the brim of his hat down.

Fran was behind the computer. Her fingers tapped away and she didn't look up: "You have no idea what it's like being around that 'See You Next Time.'"

"Fran!"

"Oh, quit being a prude. Least she didn't catch you..."

She looked up smiling, and then her eyes bugged out:

"What happened to your eye?"

"You should see the guy's fist."

She got up and stood in front of him, looking up with something like anger. "Who was it?"

"A blonde train."

She prodded at it. "Well, jump out of the way next time..."

"Ok."

"Ice?"

"Please."

Hussy sat on the waiting room sofa. Fran cracked out some ice, and wrapped the cubes in a tea towel. She passed it to him and sat down next to him.

"I told you not to get hurt."

"You told me not to die," Hussy said. "I managed that."

"Did you find anything."

"No."

"Nothing?"

He pulled his hand around his neck. "Not that I know of."

"Can't you just stop?"

"No."

"Why?"

He thought, let his hand fall to his side, then said: "Because this is what I'm supposed to do."

Fran changed tack: "What's that smell?"

"I had an incident with some air fresheners."

Fran paused, got closer and started sniffing: "No, not that. The other one. It's... RANCID." She started to gag. Her little pink tongue hung out.

Hussy took a crafty whiff of his armpit.

Fran smirked and said: "GOTCHA."

"Hmm," Hussy's expression didn't change. "Why're you still here?"

A hint of purple crossed Fran's face, but dissipated: "Research... trying to find out what the police are doing about Rick."

"Any luck?"

"Nope. Even his death hasn't been registered yet."

"How..."

Fran interrupted: "I'm good with computers." And another beautiful smile.

He knew better than to say anything more.

Fran stood up: "My car's exhaust has blown." She frowned. "Can you ride the cab with me? I hate riding alone..."

Hussy looked at his clock on the wall. He was too tired to hide it any more: "I have to be somewhere first."

"Can I come?" Then she beamed her bright white smile.

Hussy thought, calculating the pros and cons. The result was the scales were weighed evenly. He said quietly: "Ok..."

He shuffled into the cab with Fran leading him by the hand. The feel of her beautiful skin meant he fell asleep within minutes of being inside the cab.

36

Peter asked: *What did you dream?*

"It was my first memory again."

Which was?

Hussy was unsure whether he could trust the barman: "I was four years old and in pre-school. I was playing with building bricks."

And?

Now Hussy was becoming guarded and irritated: "The wall felt so big after I had finished it, even though it must have only been two feet high."

How did it make you feel?

Hussy had been a barman himself. He knew all the tricks, all the wisdom, all the empathy it brings when the alcohol releases people's true feelings: "I thought we could read minds."

I did say it doesn't work like that.

There was the slightest sense of irritation in Peter's voice.

"We're defined by what we say and do," Hussy said, "and nothing else matters."

37

"Steve!" Fran said.

"Uh?"

"Wake up, you numpty."

Hussy said: "Ah," and he slipped into the new reality.

Fran's eyes were hanging. Concern? Annoyance? "Steve, please?"

"I'm ok," he said, "honestly."

Fran watched Steve as he quietly watched how this new cabbie stared at Francesca's legs in his rear view mirror for a solid two minutes. Hussy stared at the driver's details on display. His name was Jon Smith, as nondescript as a name could be.

Smith had a loose, rubbery face. It must have been fuelled by the sourness of a job that must have infected his attitude like a thirty year old virus.

The cabbie whined: "Do you know how much they're spending on the outer harbour?"

The harbour seemed like a fine plan, and one designed so that Yarmouth could be linked to Europe. There was the possibility of a trip to Amsterdam and the joys that could bring.

"A lot?" Fran said.

"MILLIONS!" Smith groaned: "The roads'll NEVER be able to take it..."

And he ranted on and on, Hussy tuned out but watched how he kept staring at Fran's legs more than the road. He hit the side of the curb taking one corner too fast.

Hussy coughed and pointed at the rear view mirror with his eyes. Fran looked, worked it out, then winked. She carefully looked out the side, front and back windows. Then she reached down and hiked up her skirt. Only a little, and very slowly. She watched his eyes widen with his cheap little thrill.

Then Fran screamed: "WATCH OUT! CAR!"

Smith slammed on the brakes. Everyone jerked forward, clamped by their seat-belts.

Hussy looked at Fran's grin and burst into loud laughter. The cabbie looked around frantically at the completely empty side road.

He turned and glared: "WHAT THE HELL WAS THAT ABOUT?"

Fran smiled sweetly. "Maybe you should keep your eyes on the road, Rubber Johnny."

"RUBBER JOHNNY?"

"You know what I mean. Unless you want that gear shift put somewhere special." She was still beaming away.

"YOU SOME KIND OF PSYCHO?"

"Maybe."

"JESUS. YOU DO THAT AGAIN..."

Hussy said in his flat monotone: "You do what you were doing again and she will kill you."

"YOU'RE BOTH NUTS."

He pulled the car away. Smith muttered, but kept his eyes on the road.

Fran stared into Hussy's face. He was straining to open his bruised eye.

"Ouch, that thing's puffed up badly. Here..."

She put her hand next to his face and Hussy flinched.

"Hey. I'm not gonna kill you."

She stroked and prodded the swelling round the eye. It flared with heat and pain.

He said: "Ow."

"My big brave hero... I can give you some cream for that, diddums." She pulled her hand away. "If you want."

"Sure."

She reached inside her small handbag, took a dollop of some white cream and rubbed it into his eyelid.

Fran said, now whispering: "You think one of those prozzies killed Rick?"

"Prozzies?" Then he coughed a small laugh. "As if Rick would do such a thing..."

"Funn-eeeeeeeee." Fran said through gritted teeth. "They wouldn't pop off a regular, anyway."

Hussy looked up at the driver's rear view mirror and saw Jon Smith watching them carefully. He pointed his index finger at the mirror and Fran nodded...

She lowered her voice: "It was too tidy for a spur of the moment thing..."

Hussy whispered back: "The rain, the aim, the dispatch."

She feigned annoyance: "I read books, ok? I studied this stuff."

The speed – both the drug and the movement of the taxi – fired up Hussy's dozy brain. "Why you'd leave the D.A.'s?"

She snapped but still kept her voice low: "I wanted to do something on my own." Then she paused and said evenly: "Without any help from anyone."

"HEY! PSYCHO-COUPLE!" shouted Smith. "WE'RE HERE!"

Francesca looked out the front window and said: "Wow."

38

Shady Pines Retirement Community had a large forecourt surrounded by a mass of evergreen plants and trees. In the middle of the forecourt was a fountain filled with lights. Their glow chased through the water and made beautiful, looping patterns of liquid white.

The main building looked like a Tudor mansion of oak, leaded light and white stonework. It sat sturdily in the landscape like it had always been there.

Fran's mouth opened wide: "Is this your family pile?"

Hussy said: "Not quite."

"Steve, just tell me..."

They were interrupted by the bloop of the cabbie's receiver, requesting he go on another job. Smith's tone changed completely as he said: "I'll get right on it, honey."

Then the shouting started again, "GET ON WITH IT!"

Fran and Hussy responded by smiling at each other.

Now the Jon Smith raised it another notch by screaming:

Narcoleptic

"PAY AT THE SIDE."

They got out. Slowly. It was still damn cold and the wind whistled through the needles on the pines.

Hussy went around to his window and smiled at him. Francesca followed.

The cabbie had a silly little sawn-off in his hands. How did these people get hold of guns?

Hussy's fully open eye sagged: "A baby gun."

"NOT SO CHATTY NOW, HEY? GIVE ME THE FARE OR I'LL KILL YOU." Smith nodded over to the meter.

"Cute gun," Hussy said. "Just lemme get my money out."

"DON'T MOVE."

"I'll pay," said Fran.

"YOU EITHER."

It was very easy for Hussy to say: "How about I stick my fingers in your little gun?" He shoved two fingers into the barrels. "I can still get my money with my free hand."

"YOU'RE CRAZY. I'LL BLOW YOUR HAND OFF."

"No, you won't."

Hussy reached down and pulled the trigger with his free hand. The gun made a fake rattling sound and the end glowed red. A phony gun, a child's toy.

Hussy peeled off the two notes, and drew out the exact change from his pocket. He emptied it onto the cabbie's lap.

Now the cabbie looked shocked: "Where's the tip?"

"Buy porn," said Fran.

"And drive safely," Hussy said.

Francesca and Hussy started to walk off. Francesca walked in front of him. He felt like a superhero.

"YOU'RE CRAZY!" Jon Smith shouted as he pulled away. "YOU HEAR ME?!"

They heard him, didn't look back and they kept walking.

Fran flipped him the finger as Hussy trailed behind, stifling laughter.

39

Through the big double doors, behind the desk, there was Mrs. Devgan. She was there every weekday evening. She was tired looking, her hips were spread apart and she had a jaded face that had seen everything and too much. She was like another piece of the furniture, only in a blue uniform and pretty brown skin. She was a lovely human being.

Hussy said: "Hello, Mrs. Devgan."

"Hello, Mr. Hussy." Then she turned to Fran: "Hello, madam."

"Hi!" said Fran.

"How's Mum been today?"

Fran shoved his back when he said: "Mum," and she whispered *"Why didn't you tell me..."*

"Fine, Mr. Hussy." Mrs. Devgan went on, in her clipped

voice, "She's in her room now."

"Thanks. Can I have a word later?"

"Certainly, Mr. Hussy. I'll see you soon."

"Ready?" Hussy said to Fran.

"For you to introduce me to your mother?"

He sighed. He suspected she thought this was a goof. "Be patient, alright?"

She kept leading the way, despite not knowing where she was going.

"Room 10, ok?" He said, and she looked around at signs.

"These carpets are beautiful and thick," said Fran, admiring them. Her heels made no sound on them.

"I could totally sleep on 'em!" Her head was on a swivel. "This whole place is beautiful. Those paintings. All the wood. All the space... Wow. What did your mum do? Defence lawyer?"

"She was a writer."

She stopped still and glared at him: "Why didn't you say before?"

"You never asked."

They both turned when they heard laughter, and looked through some windows into what his mother called "The Goldfish Bowl." Inside was the dining area, where small, neatly arranged elderly people were eating their supper. There were large round round tables with dainty white tablecloths.

One nurse was cleaning food off the ground. She was chatting happily with the elderly dude who had dropped it.

Through the glass they could hear the dude say loudly: "I'm dreadfully sorry." Hussy knew he had been a writer too.

A handsome male nurse came out with more wine. The dapper dude chugged it back, and then repeated his apology.

"I want to live here, please," said Francesca, half-smiling. The male nurse bent over to serve someone. He was carved from marble and polished to Grecian perfection.

"I bet you do," Hussy said. "Come on."

They reached the small window in the door of Room 10. Hussy pointed at it and said: "That's Mum."

She was fifty-nine years old and she looked ten years younger. Fire still blazed in her red-brown eyes. The only resemblance to Hussy was her dark, curly hair. She had deep brown skin and age hadn't taken away her full, black lips. In her day, she had been revered as a beauty and the surface had changed surprising little over the years.

"That's your mum?" Fran's eyes had widened fully.

"That is my mum."

Patricia Hussy was in her comfy chair and engrossed in playing Solitaire with her well-worn cards on the same lap-tray.

She played 2 draw, 1 time through. Very quick but practically impossible to get out. A TV flickered in the corner, but it was silent. A cup of tea sat on a table next to the chair. Her meds were next to it.

Hussy looked at Fran and said: "Be nice."

"Hey!" Francesca looked offended.

"Sorry. Just be yourself."

She stuck out her tongue: "I was going to be Madonna."

Hussy opened the door and followed her in.

40

Hussy's mother had been a recognised genius. Her face had been on the cover on *The Guardian*, *The Spectator*, *The Independent* and more. She'd narrowly missed out on being *Time Magazine*'s Person of the Year. Hussy had seen how angry she was about that...

Her views on race – starting in the 70s writing about being a child of the Windrush generation – had been far ahead of their time. Humanity was finally catching up, but it still had years – probably decades – to go before the mainstream would comprehend the truth. There were too many distractions in the Middle East and the economy for the powers-that-weren't to think about such complex matters as humanism.

They say the fire the burns twice as bright, burns oh-so-brightly... and Patricia Hussy had burned so very brightly. Luckily, Patricia's dementia merely exaggerated the core truths she had always felt.

Patricia looked up at them as they entered the room. She waved her hand to say: "Wait," and her long black fingers went back to her game of Patience.

Francesca sat in the pale yellow chair near the door. She had a happy, inquisitive look. She crossed her legs and quietly tapped the heel of one knee boot into the side of the other.

Hussy glanced down and smiled, and Fran saw it. She mouthed "What?" but didn't say it.

He mouthed: "Nothing" and went over to the TV in the corner. A repeat was playing. A young rich lawyer was pouting and moaning about how terrible her life was. This scene featured her breasts growing to CGI monstrosities in her bathroom mirror.

Hussy flicked it off, and the silence was pleasant again.

"Close shave," Patricia said. She hadn't got out again.

Hussy said: "I've never seen you get out. It's pretty much impossible."

"It's a challenge." She put the cards in a stack, and Fran watched – mute. "It's like climbing a mountain. You get there in the end..."

Now she stared at him.

"Yeah, I'm late," he had been conditioned to sense and dart around her moods, "it was the traffic... Sorry."

"Are you ok?" Her face shifted as she looked closer. His swollen one could still only open halfway. "What's that?"

"Nothing."

"It's something."

"Hmm."

"Learn to speak your mind."

"Hmm."

She narrowed her eyes at him and then turned towards Fran. Her eyes blazed with happiness.

"Hello, beautiful friend," she said.

"Hiya, Mrs. Hussy," said Fran. "I'm Francesca. I'm Steve's secretary." She offered her hand for a shake.

"What a beautiful name for a beautiful woman." She could get away with that sort of line, and she looked deep into Fran's eyes when she shook it. Patricia decoded some mystery that only she could see.

"Uh," Fran said. "Thank you."

"I've learned to tell the truth whenever I can," Patricia said. "When we're gone, what's left except the that?"

Hussy adjusted the tightness in his neck once again. He said: "Nothing" to finish the quote from his mother's second book: *The Rush Wound Around Us All.*

"Would you like a drink?" Patricia offered. "There's some orange in the fridge." She laughed: "It's cold as a witch's teat."

"Fran?"

"OK, slave-driver..." Fran said, and then winked at Patricia. Patricia smiled and Hussy dutifully went to the kitchen and poured out three glasses.

He served up the two glasses of orange juice and then downed his own glass.

"Rick was murdered last night," Hussy said.

"Rick?" Patricia said, with something like a smirk on her face. "That child with the gammy eye?"

"No," Hussy said. "My partner."

Confusion set in and she looked stunned: "Well... Stephen, if you'd told me it wouldn't have been an issue..."

"Detective partner," said Fran. She made a tiny throaty laugh but held the rest back.

"Oh, HIM." Thoughts dashed into Patricia's head, but they could only survive for minutes: "You didn't like him anyway."

"No..."

"A pus-filled boil on the anus of humanity, you said." Now her smile had spread fully over her face. "I remember stuff like that."

Fran made another little noise.

"My brain's like a sponge," Patricia grinned but the way her teeth ceased to fit looked so unlike how she used to be.

"We're trying to solve the murder," said Fran.

The same look in response: "When life gives you lemons, make lemonade."

"I think my lemons have dried up, Mum," Hussy said.

"You should get some ointment for that," said Fran.

Patricia and Fran smiled... Partners in crime.

"How've you been, Mum?"

"Oh, you know." Her mood changed visibly. "Just fine. Like the weather."

"You sure?"

"YES," she pulled her black hair through four fingers on her left hand. "Just catching up on some foot-dangling."

There was silence for a half minute. Like all silences, it felt much longer. The absence of noise can make the normal person go insane. It's why people dream and it's why they stifle thought with movies and music and TV. Little games to hide from true thought.

Patricia was the first to speak: "It's not often I get to see a woman like you any more..." Then she pulled through her beautiful afro once again. "And your name?"

"Francesca Dawn," Fran said.

There was a strangeness to Patricia's eyes: "Such a beautiful name for a beautiful woman..."

Fran blushed: "Thank-you."

"Like the sun rising..." And once again she tailed off and now kneaded her forehead.

Hussy was too attuned to this: "You need to rest, Mum."

She spoke loudly: "I KNOW."

"Fran," Hussy said, quietly. "Can you call us a cab?"

His mother overheard and brightened, her eyes like a switch turned on. "I hope you wouldn't mind if I had a word with Stephen," she said. "Family things. I don't want to bore you..."

"Of course... Patricia." Fran got up, got her hand kissed by Patricia, and smiled broadly.

Hussy fished around in his pocket for a different taxi firm. He hated travelling with the same driver repeatedly – unless it was Shubey – and he had no desire to form any relationship with those that required him to talk too much.

Fran said: "Bye, beautiful," and kissed his mother's hand. "I'll be out front, ok?" Francesca left and they both watched her leave.

"You're in love, aren't you." It wasn't a question. Patricia looked at him, reducing him to an adolescent.

"Hmm." His eyebrows lowered.

Patricia harped: "Give it a few years and it might wear off."

They looked at each other for ten seconds or so. Blue eyes meeting brown eyes.

Patricia said: "She doesn't realise she's the beautiful one."

"You're crazy. She has to."

"Maybe... Maybe she just likes sparkling sapphire eyes."

"Your eyes are brown."

"Exactly."

"What does that mean?"

Patricia smiled at that: "You might still catch her if you hurry."

"I'm not a kid."

"You are sometimes. Everyone is."

Something briefly softened in his mother's eyes. Something before she had become an idol for so many people. Even though she didn't remember much of that time, she had been a great mother with terrible taste in men.

"Good guys always win in the end," Patricia said.

"Mum..." Then he sighed: "They don't."

Hussy got up as she loudly said: "Be YOU, always BE YOU."

"I'll see you tomorrow."

And his mother had to get the last word: "You better."

Hussy shut the door gently, and stood behind it for a few seconds and moved on to whatever new hell awaited him.

41

Along the corridor, Hussy could hear giggling. It got louder as he went along. When he reached reception Francesca and Mrs. Devgan stopped.

Mrs. Devgan was suppressing a laugh. Hussy had never seen her *smile* before.

Hussy raised an eyebrow and said: "Hello."

Mrs. Devgan's demeanour returned: "Hello, Mr. Hussy."

Fran smiled and said: "Cab's on its way. Woman's voice."

"Good."

"Couldn't be any worse than the last perve..."

Mrs. Devgan laughed a tiny, mouse-like titter: "I've got your card caboodle ready, Mr. Hussy."

Caboodle? A very Fran-like word.

He went back to the desk and sorted out payment through the card. He signed the same forms he always had to sign.

"Francesca," whispered Mrs. Devgan, "is a lovely girl..."

"I know..." They exchanged goodbyes.

A toot of a horn from outside. The rain and wind were in a temporary lull. They settled into the back seat of the cab as the female driver turned around with a sweet smile from a kindly face: "Where to, mah dahl-lins?" Her Norfolk accent was beautiful and lilted, and her name-tag was marked as Joey Frye.

Fran told her the address and smiled.

Frye pulled away and drove with the elegance of a getaway driver, coaxing her cab through the drying streets with practised ease.

Hussy could feel the atmosphere in the car.

"Steve," and Fran turned earnestly towards him: "Were you adopted?"

The question had been answered so many times: "No."

"But..." And Fran smiled her beautiful smile.

"She's my mother," Hussy said, trying to brighten. "She's a pain in the backside, but you didn't know how she was before."

Fran paused, then said: "I bet she could solve anything."

He coughed his strange laugh: "Maybe..."

"Steve..." Fran started.

Hussy cut in: "My mother has early onset dementia."

"Not that. I know that... Steve, she's lovely."

"I know."

"Why didn't you say you were adopted? Steve, it doesn't..."

He cut in again: "Because I wasn't adopted."

"But..."

He shut both eyes tight and squeezed the bridge of his nose again.

"I have," and Hussy almost spat the words, "what idiots call 'passing complexion.'"

She poked his arm: "Ok." She beamed her bright white smile again. "Why so grumpy?"

"Because I inherited all of my deadbeat father's looks and only some of my mother's brains."

Fran's smile waned somewhat: "You did ok..."

"Fran... don't..."

She hugged his arm and Hussy tensed in response. This was something new. It was terrifying.

The cab slowed gracefully to a stop. "We're 'ere mah dears," was followed by an even kinder smile from the driver.

The apartment building was nondescript and so unlike Fran.

"Steve..." She looked into his one and a half eyes. "Thanks, boss."

"Hmm."

Fran insisted on paying.

"Fran..."

"Pfffft... And here's a hug." She wrapped around all of his body now. A beautfiul, comforting blanket. She said: "Don't do anything crazy tonight, ok?"

"As if..."

Narcoleptic

"We'll figure stuff about Rick tomorrow, ok?"

"We will."

She kissed his forehead and left.

Hussy eased back in his seat with a bemused grin.

"Cloud Nine, please," he asked the driver.

"I thought so!" She winked in the rear mirror.

"Uh-huh."

He fell asleep for five minutes but whatever dream he had was lost in the ether.

"WE'RE 'ERE M'DEAR," the driver shouted, and smiled as she turned around to face him.

"Thanks...."

"Say hi to Em for me."

Hahaha... "I will." Then he handed over thirty quid, which included a fifty percent tip.

"Hush money, huh, love?" and Joey Frye laughed...

42

Cloud Nine opened at nine o'clock, so wandering in ten minutes after that wasn't best practice. It smacked of desperation.

The cube-bodied doorman asked for ten quid and said: "Don't touch the girls. Keep your hands behind you at all times."

Hussy's blank face looked forward: "Of course..."

Narcoleptic

He had arrived as the strippers were milling around, drinking at the bar and talking. He half-caught conversations about their madam as he looked at the empty pole and drank. He didn't want to talk to them. He just wanted to see them.

It was a strip joint but the girls weren't going to dance on stage for one sucker. They moped about and looked at Hussy with a mixture of confusion and disgust. They talked to the barman. Then they looked at Hussy and laughed quietly.

He downed the remainder of his watered down beer. Then he went into the toilets, took out his hipflask and took a long slug of expensive Bison Grass vodka. The bison knew what they were doing when they urinated in the Bialowieza Forest...

He wandered out and sat in the corner. He was thirty feet away from the stage, and none of the strippers came and sat with him.

Hussy thought about Rick to stop thinking about Francesca. Rick had liked strip joints, but Hussy had always been wary of them.

Of course, Rick loved to spout his cock-eyed philosophy: "All women are prostitutes," Rick had started. "You know that?"

"What?"

Once again, he puffed out his barrel chest. "All women are prostitutes."

Hussy had paused, then said: "Why?"

"First, you've got hookers. At least they know what they are." The leer spread across Rick's face. "They give you some good times for money. Mmm-mmm." This routine was clearly practised, refined to some pathetic speech. "Second, you've got gold diggers. They make it pretty obvious what they're after. They go after rich guys, even if they're old or ugly or stupid. That's fair enough as long as they don't make out they're in love. I think of it as a reward for making the money in the first place." How did this explain his latest partner? He acted outside but he was as inside as most of humankind. "Third, you've got wives and girlfriends and lovers. They're the worst because they put out the least."

Hussy looked forward, desperate for a drink and some ear plugs: "But you got married... twice..."

Again, no reaction, Acton was on a tedious roll: "You get a wife and you end up buying them stuff to get some action. Birthday presents. Other presents. Meals, movies, clothes... a house. You ever see a women willing to pay for a guy?"

"Occasionally..."

"Exactly." Acton continued to ramble: "They know what they're doing. So they bleed us guys dry."

"Us?" Hussy's fists were clenching yet again.

"They don't even know they're prostitutes," Acton finally deflated his barrel chest and sank back into his seat, "but they are."

Hussy looked at a pathetic creature and said: "You're a real romantic."

"I just know how things stand." Acton's fingers needed

something to do so he rolled a cigarette.

"I've known women better than that," Hussy said.

"You get any action?"

"Not much."

"I'll lend you some money if you want."

"Nah..."

"You know where I am, buddy."

Buddy?

The memory faded and Hussy walked automatically to the bar and bought two doubles of tolerable vodka with ice.

The women watched him come and watched him go.

He sat back down in his corner spot and one of them decided to come over. She was 20-ish, with blonde frizzy hair and long legs. She had a misaligned nose that bent one way, and Hussy found it very sexy. She also had high heels and an evening gown in red sequins.

"Hi, I'm Cassandra," she said. "You look lonely."

"Just waiting on a friend."

"Oh, yeah?"

"Rick Acton. You know him?" Hussy asked. "Short, thin, stinky. Comes in here a lot."

"Rick... No... Sorry." The way she moved her eyes told him a lot. "Do you want to buy me a drink?"

"Not really."

She acted hurt. "Oh, purr-lease." And she ran her hand down his right thigh.

A meanness came over Hussy, and he hated himself for it: "The amount of money you earn you should be buying me a drink."

She glared at him with pretty, heavily made-up eyes: "Don't you like me? Don't you like the way I look?"

Hussy's suddenly cold, dead eyes stared forward: "You're an incredibly attractive woman."

She didn't know how to take that: "I'll loosen up after a drink or two."

He wasn't in the mood. "That'd be water retention."

"Maybe I should come back after you've had a few more." She slid off the chair. A long slit ran up the middle of her skirt reaching her bellybutton giving a tantalising glimpse of lace underwear. "I'll be waiting," she said. "Think about me."

"I will."

At 20, Hussy thought didn't need anyone. At 25, he was almost dribbling into a bib over Francesca. By the time if – and it was a big if – he hit his forties, Hussy feared he would become Rick. A needy little sucker who had his pathetic needs dealt with like antiseptic on a wound.

Cassandra shimmied back to her colleagues. She whispered, and they acted sympathetic. But the derision was plain to see, and Hussy watched that too.

The place started to fill up. The girls spread out amongst the clientèle. Some went through to the "other room" with them. Every ten minutes one of them would dance on stage in their advertising slot.

They had a voucher system going. You bought a voucher from the bar. 15 for one dancer, 25 for two. Hussy watched and drank.

The pole dances lasted about 3 minutes. The length of a song the lady had picked. Some revealed the bizarrely sacred ground of nipples. Some did not.

Before the dances, the men had that over-happy grin plastered on their face. Then, afterwards, they had a jaded look that made Hussy smile. More suckers, and no different from him.

If you had vouchers he noticed the women would crowd around you. Some guys gave one girl more than one voucher. He guessed that these men got to choose from the specials board.

Rick fitted into this world all too perfectly. Seedy, predatory eyes, a lost-looking gaze and a little drool. Hussy, on the other hand, continued to drink and watch. Most people he saw were in groups. Annoying and stupid and fake and loud.

Hussy bought more vodka and Cloud Nine's barman had no information. He was too busy trying to flirt with the women, and Hussy knew it was time to move on.

He walked to the next club. There were only three strip clubs in Yarmouth. Cloud Nine, The Smut Hut, and Destiny's.

The girls already started to look the same in Destiny's. A brush back of hair and hair extensions, heavy eye make-up, a practised smile and sparkling lipstick.

They also sounded the same. A nasal "Hey baby" greeted

him in each place from the women now eager for private dances to cover their pole fee. They tried to maintain eye contact with him, but he could sense their secret disgust at his face.

The artifice was exactly the opposite of what Hussy wanted, but it was exactly what made them appeal to the white faces that glowed in the UV light and throbbing noise. As the night had moved on, the smell of sweaty men and cheap perfume was noxious.

Hussy thought of the Mr. Airplane Man song called "Red Light."

The beautiful, wonky nosed singer had sung:

Oh baby, hold me tight.

C'mon baby, turn on your red light.

And he managed, somehow, to stay awake.

Or, at least, he always felt as if he was awake.

43

Hussy ordered a triple of sweet Irish whiskey and drank it. Then he bought a beer to tide him over.

As he sipped it, an unbidden thought floated into his head... He knew he would kill for Francesca. Not out of misguided violence. But to protect her, no matter what.

He stretched out his hands, checking to see whether they shook or not. Fat half-moon shapes sat at the base of each

Narcoleptic

fingernail. White with only the hint of corrosion and yellow pitting at the top of them.

The guy next to him looked like a fellow drinker, prematurely old and tired. Grey dirty beard, drawn face, big red nose. A thin open shirt that was held together with stains.

"Hey," Hussy said to him.

"Screw you," he said back.

Hussy smiled, and went back to his beer.

He sat there thinking about Francesca. She was another puzzle that he would fail to solve.

Now another waking dream. His eyes were open, but the room almost muted and the images quavered into a blur.

"Steve," Fran had said, "Are you attracted to women?"

"Yes," he was affronted, "I like them a great deal."

"So?"

"So," and he smiled, "what?"

"So why don't you do anything about it?"

Hussy shut his eyes and then opened them. Then his mind said: "Because it will happen when it's meant to."

That made her laugh and Francesca's figure and face shifted again. Sometimes blonde, sometimes brunette, always beautiful: "How terribly Zen!"

"Who's this Zen character?"

Then she prodded him under his ribcage, wrapped herself around him again. They fitted neatly together... this tall outsider and this short, curvy woman. He could swear she had shrunk...

but maybe because she was out of her heels? Even Fran's voice sounded different. Slurred? But it was still Fran...

He lifted her up as she grabbed around him. She locked her arms around his neck and her legs clamped around his waist as he lifted her backside.

"Imma koala!"

"Yup!"

"Let's see how far you can walk with me around you!"

So Hussy smiled and walked, looking into Fran's shifting face as she giggled. He felt utter joy.

When he fully woke up, the guy at the bar had left.

Hussy ordered another whiskey and the barman saw his distant face, poured a triple whiskey, and wandered off.

Yet more detective work had been a nonsensical waste of time and energy. There was only one strip club left.

Hussy shut his eyes and he wanted to sleep again.

44

"I better have another drink here too," Hussy asked Peter. "This stuff is non-alcoholic. isn't it?"

Not quite.

"It's tasty enough..."

Peter polished a glass. Movement always seemed to force thought into people's heads. A tiny rush of blood that pulled them out of the sedentary mindset.

Are you a misogynist?

"No." For the first time, Hussy was riled. "Most women have a lot more to offer, personality wise." He downed another glass of the ruby wine. "They think more." His attitude had become surly: "Tell me what it's called when you hate guys?"

Sorry. No idea.

"Weird that..." He waited as his glass was refillled. He was like a engine that needed alcohol as fuel. Now he was in the equivalent of fifth gear. "I hate men, but with women it's different. There are idiot women too, of course. But even the good ones are closed off to me. Don't let him get too close... what would he do? He MUST want me... He's ugly... He must be crazy too... Run... Treat him bad..."

Peter let something like a sigh out... *Humans are mostly lovely. Try to step back.*

Hussy went on: "Maybe. Maybe not. I'm hardly delusional about my appeal." He rubbed the back of his head. "Francesca, she was lovely. Maybe a few others, once. It's rare." Another glass sunk down his mouth, no desire to taste the wine but the need to have it inside him. "I could be wrong. I could've been paranoid. I doubt it."

So why do you need to drink? To escape?

Hussy looked startled by that. "I just wanted it. It used to dull everything. But the more you drink, the more you need to dull everything. Don't drink enough and you just feel bad more intensely. But I never fancied the gutter." He held up the wine glass: "Is this stuff expensive?"

Not really.

"Got to be cheaper than the stuff in those strip joints..." He trailed off: "...can I have another glass?"

Take the bottle. It might help.

"The word is misandry," Hussy said, "by the way." He tightly gripped the bottle of dry red wine in his right hand. "And I'm misabstinent..."

45

The last strip club – the beautifully named "Smut Hut" – was doing OK. Most of the tables were full. The men were sitting around, drinking and talking to the women and to each other. They were buying the women drinks.

Hussy remained seated alone. He'd walked down a flight of stairs to get into the place, and it felt like he was descending into some sleazy hell.

The word "Francesca" pounded in his head. Just the word had an endless beauty.

One table drew Hussy's attention because it was quiet. Three men, all in grey suits, one woman in a silver twinset.

A skinny guy who twitched too much, a beefcake blond man with a gimpy eye, a big black bald guy, and a woman too old

Narcoleptic

and too sad for this life. The Tall Man and The Goon, with two pals.

The big guy got up and went into the "other room."

Courage and stupidity are fine margins. Hussy tried to gauge the situation as much as his foggy brain would allow. So he walked over and said: "Hello."

The three of them looked at him as if he had crawled out from under a fresh turd. The Tall Man dismissed him with a sniff and the Goon looked, a leaden blob of flesh covering so little inside.

"Hello?" Hussy drew up his spine and smiled.

Tall Man said: "You looking for the loser's convention?"

The woman laughed.

Hussy said: "Looks like I found it."

Goon reached for his pocket.

Hussy said: "Don't move."

"What is your concern, friend?" Tall Man asked.

"Answer my questions and we'll go from there."

They looked through him. Tall Man and the woman smiled, and the Goon just stared.

Hussy said: "Don't think you'll get me wi..."

Hussy felt a hot liquid flush inside the back of his head.

A black hole engulfed him, but he entered it with a practised serenity.

46

Another dream floated into Hussy's head. Although he couldn't move, he knew it was because he wasn't dead.

He was back in High School. The Geography teacher taught about mountains in Uganda and farming methods in Zaire.

The teacher used same words over and over again: "fairly obviously" and "concerned."

"Fairly obviously," and he glared at a podgy female student, "I am concerned with your behaviour."

And more: "Zaire is concerned with its crops, obviously." Then he prodded at a young, topless black man with a hoe.

"It's fairly obvious that clouds are something that concern us all." Now there was an image of a stormy sky. "Climate change is somewhat of a hoax, in that the reality is something far, far worse than your minds can imagine..."

Hussy would sit there and keep score. One column for "obviously," one for the "concerned." He would plot them on graphs, and work out how many the teacher said per lesson.

After a few weeks, Hussy showed the teacher all of the graphs he had made.

The teacher looked at them and said: "Hmm." His face blurred between the gap-toothed teacher of Hussy's past, and The Tall Man. The result was a strange, almost troll-like creature.

In the next lesson the teacher didn't say "obviously" or "concerned" once. But the lesson after that – sped up somehow

Narcoleptic

in Hussy's dream – the teacher was back off again saying "fairly obviously" and "concerned" in almost every sentence...

It was the smell that brought him back to consciousness. The room smelled like the teacher's breath. Rotten eggs, spoiled fruit, damp cabbage, parmesan cheese and over-stewed coffee. All of them were mixed together for the full death-breath effect.

Hussy opened his eyes, but the room was pitch black and almost silent. He could feel the air was heavy and wet. His head felt like shards of glass and he ached for another drink. Thin rope dug into his hands, and they were tied to the back of the chair.

He could feel his sleep paralysis. He was aware of being frozen but he had no idea of how he could end it.

God, god, he needed a drink.

There was a quiet, consistent tapping noise. Tap, tap, tap... then taptaptaptap... then back to tap, tap, tap.

Chinese water torture is more consistent than that, isn't it? He would have moaned but his lips wouldn't move.

Hussy waited. He would need to urinate soon and the shakes were starting. A gurgling in his stomach, the need to vomit or defecate.

After thirty minutes, maybe hours, his twitching eyes saw a thin line of light to his right, low down. Feet on the other side of the door. Now more light. Now the creak of the door opening.

He knew the DT's were kicking in, and he knew he had to escape to get some alcohol inside him.

The door opened and he registered what he could when

Narcoleptic

the light blasted in. Three men blotted it out as they strode inside.

His room had no windows. His chair was wooden and bolted to the ground. Hussy squinted into the light from the open door. His shirt and stab-proof vest had been stripped off him.

Goon said: "He's just sitting there, boss."

The Tall Man said: "You obviously expected him to be dancing the tango?"

Baldy looked forward and only the woman was missing from their reunion.

Still taptaptaptap... Then the moth flew out from the strip light. Baldy came forward and caught it with a giant CLAP. He rubbed the dust off his hands.

The Tall Man stood in front of Hussy. Baldy and Goon were posted in the two corners facing him.

"Who are you?" said The Tall Man.

Hussy was struck by odd things he not noticed before. Like himself, The Tall Man had very black curly hair. But unlike Hussy, his shoes were small given his height. Maybe a size 6? He carried no presence, and Hussy would have broken his neck if he had been given the chance.

"Sffffffhhsss," Hussy replied.

"He can't talk correctly," said Baldy.

Hussy said: "Fffffoooo."

"Drunk, I bet," said Goon.

"What's up with his face?" The Tall Man cocked his head

Narcoleptic

to one side. He was so thin he could have slid under the crack of a door.

Goon said: "Probably a train wreck."

The Tall Man giggled like a woman. "Sober him up, boys." Then he exited with something like a saunter.

Hussy said after him: "Ssssfffffff!"

Baldy and Goon slapped him around. He thought about booze the whole time, and felt very little of the pain.

"Not too much on the face," Goon said. "We don't want to make him pretty, do we?"

Hussy noted that Goon was still limping on the leg he'd kicked. He stared at the leg and shouted: "HAAAAAAAAH!"

Goon went for a kidney a couple of times. Baldy gave him a couple more shots to his face. A tooth came loose. Blood flowed out of his nose he could feel tar-like liquid in his mouth.

He spat out what was in there, but laughed through cracked lips and his cataplexy: "Ffffffffoooo!"

Hussy was drowning in his face, but with each blow the paralysis wore off. His hands worked silently at the rope around his hands. He could feel them cutting in, but that was ok...

Goon said: "Right, that'll do."

Hussy spat out the tooth. A molar. He'd looked after that sucker, too. "Fanks," he gurgled. "Who needs surge...ery?"

Goon laughed. "So you're a Hussy then?"

"Iamwhutlam," and his smile was stained with blood.

Goon looked at Baldy, then came over and gave Hussy

another bop on the nose. It cracked.

"Well dun." Another smile. "You'd mmmmissed dat."

The psychopaths looked at each other and the Goon spoke: "Well, Hussy. I'm Thomas Salter. Heard of me?"

"Yesssss," seemed like the wise reply.

"Good. The nigger is called Tyrone."

Tyrone drew himself up and twisted his neck to one side.

Hussy glared at Salter furiously and said: "A'right, untie me an' dis time I'll properleeee kick yer backside, you ****."

"In your dreams..." Salter pointed at Tyrone and said: "If you see him, you know you're dead."

"Ah," Hussy burbled. "But if ya dun kill me, I'll kill yoooo."

Tyrone set his neck straight again and bopped Hussy on the nose. But it was so much lighter than before. Tyrone said: "Pay attention, please, Mr. Hussy."

He caught his breath. "Can ya do th' uvver cheek next time?" And he spat out more blood. "I like symmetry."

More silent attempts to loosen the rope and another slap from Salter.

Hussy said: "I wanna know 'bout Rick Acton."

"Who?"

"Rick... Ac... ton."

Tyrone said: "Who is he?"

"Izza private 'tective."

Salter said: "So?"

Oh no... he could see it in their eyes: "You've nevva met

him, 'ave you?"

"No..."

Hussy sighed and Salter looked confused: "Why'd you come to us?"

"He got," Hussy spat out yet more blood, "killed."

"Are you a cop or something?"

"Nah," Hussy said, "I sell hats." Tyrone smiled at that, and Hussy knew they weren't lying: "Why were ya at 'is place?"

Salter cocked his head to one side again: "It was empty."

"Yer jus' thieves?"

"Well, basically..." Salter looked affronted. "Is that it?"

"Yep," Hussy said, "I'll be on ma way den."

"How?"

"Untie me." And he pulled another bloodied smile.

Tyrone said in monotone: "I don't want to kill him."

Something like concern passed over Salter's face: "You're a hitman, it's what you do..." He punched Hussy in the ribcage.

But now Tyrone pushed him back and said: "We will just booze him up and dump him..."

Hussy smiled again, feeling his teeth before he opened his mouth again: "Why?"

Tyrone's face moved in a way Hussy couldn't decipher. "No-one will believe you anyway." What was that look? Compassion? Boredom? Tyrone pulled back Salter's hand as he drew back for another punch, and he said: "Because I know."

He switched his hands to Salter's head and twisted them.

Narcoleptic

There was the tiniest noise, like a piece of popcorn opening. Tyrone then gently held Salter to the ground where he laid dead.

"You need to live," the black man stared at Hussy.

"Why?"

Tyrone looked silently to his left and up high. Hussy craned his neck around... it was a filthy wall-mounted cupboard. Tyrone pulled out cheap booze and a funnel.

He put the funnel into Hussy's mouth and poured down the liquor. It wasn't enough to make him vomit, but it was enough to make him drunk.

Hussy stopped shaking. It was a twisted relief.

Tyrone gently raised up Hussy's chin and his deep brown eyes looked into Hussy's strange blue eyes. Tyrone said: "Forget this foolishness," and he ran his hands through Hussy's curly hair.

Hussy burbled and he was already starting to fall asleep: "Peachessssssss unnnn creeeeam..."

Now more darkness, no voices, and the feel of the movement of a car and lights above. The car stank of sticky, cloying death. Salter's corpse was resting heavily against him to his left, and The Tall Man's corpse was slumped over Salter's groin.

Tyrone said: "You are awake, then?" He looked back at Hussy over the arch of his driver's headrest. He slammed his fist into the Tall Man's corpse: "He was called Ricardo..."

"Yssssss."

"I will leave you with Fran, ok?"

"Hoooooow?"

Tyrone said, flatly. "Take care, my friend."

He opened the back door of the car silently, and gently lifted Hussy onto the pavement. He moved smoothly towards the door and knocked once.

Hussy teetered at the doorway as Tyrone placed Hussy's fedora on his head and said: "May the hat bring you good luck."

Tyrone turned, lit up the car's engine, and rolled serenely towards the sand and the endless water of Yarmouth's coast.

Hussy dropped to his knees, fell down and fell asleep.

47

Hussy's next memory was Francesca standing in the light.

He shut and opened his eyes and suddenly Fran was 5'2", busty and blonde. Hussy shook his head and she returned to normal. Then she shouted: "STEVE!"

The concept of death bored Hussy, but Fran was life. She embodied movement, action and wonder.

Her body glowed in the light. A cute satin red crop-top and blue hipster jeans. A bellybutton too. He loved it.

"Innnnnnie," Hussy garbled.

Her mouth was in an O. Her hair was back in a ponytail.

She was the most beautiful of humankind, indescribable but radiating heat. She held him up and shouted: "WHAT DID

YOU DO?!"

"Bllllll. Uddd..." Hussy mumbled. "I tried to cccc-cuck-cuck-clean..."

Then he drifted into a dream with only a pinprick of light telling him he was not quite dead. True death would be empty of sound and light and memory... the ultimate truth of mankind.

There were dreams of convulsions, then the realisation that they were real. He tried to stop them and he wasn't able to.

Again the image of Fran being so much shorter and white-skinned peppered his fevered thoughts.

Now there was a sofa under him and a blanket over him. Fran's hand stroked through his hair. More convulsions, but Hussy shook and laughed wildly throughout the rest of them.

She rested her hand on his forehead. She said: "You're an idiot," then kissed his nose.

He croaked out: "I... now..." Then he corrected himself: "KNOW... Know... know..."

His throat felt like razorblades. The gap in his mouth where the tooth was missing fascinated him. It seemed huge against his tongue.

He tried to move his limbs. Legs, arms, toes, fingers... all working. But his hat... where was his hat? He scratched his ugly, white head. His left forefinger drew blood.

Hussy looked around the room. Fran had a big framed original poster of *The Hitch-Hiker* on the wall.

"Hitch..." he mumbled. "Ida..."

He didn't know she'd seen that. There was the usual other stuff: TV, pictures, polished floorboards, table, a couple of comfy chairs. A neon clock – 6.12am.

The earth was quiet as Hussy looked under his blanket. His clothes had gone but he had underwear on. It was clean, white and it had lace on on it. He laughed and croaked: "Comfy."

Every movement felt like pain as he puffed air in and out. He bolted upright. He knew the moment when a friendship ended was when the respect ended.

"LIE DOWN, YOU IDIOT," said Francesca, and tapped his nose. "You're okay," And she laughed a little too: "Okay?"

"Don't..." and Hussy's body tensed. "Please go away."

There were puce bruises over his stomach and sides, and his chest was bound up tightly. His livid skin showed though, riddled with psoriasis. Black hair shot out here and there from his chest and his arms poked out like calloused branches of a tree.

"You're not going to blow chunks again, are you?"

"Have I been puking?" Of course he had. He could still taste the bile.

"Just for a few hours..."

"I can't remember," he said. "I'm so sorry."

"I had to hose you down," Fran said, "in the tub."

"Just shoot me," then a pause that said much more than words. He strained to move his body upright. Then he laughed, something like a choke rather than anything pure.

"Steve," Fran said, and he could see how her attitude had

changed, "don't worry, ok?"

His skin had turned interesting colours in places. Green, purple, black, red, yellow, blue. A rainbow. Some colours broke in the middle and a little blood leaked out.

Fran rubbed in some more grey cream. Her touch was firm but soft.

"Who did this, Steve?"

"Some friendly gangsters."

"Which ones?"

"Thomas..." He fumbled for the other name: "Ricardo?"

"It's on the news... and you've just named them."

"What?"

"They found their body parts on the beach."

"What?"

"Cooked in cheap booze... and absolutely no evidence."

Her eyebrows raised in the middle.

"Fran," Hussy said, "I didn't kill them."

"Steve..." She glared, and her lips wavered. "You could've got killed too."

"Oh, well."

Her laugh came from nowhere. "You're such an idiot." Then she rasped: "Drink your coffee."

"Can I have my hat?"

She got up and chucked his hat at him. "Here you are, hat-boy."

"Fran."

"What?"

"Fran... they didn't kill Rick."

"WHAT?"

"I know they didn't. I felt it."

"So what do we do?"

"Can you see the D.A.?"

"This is stupid."

"Please. Just ask around."

"WHY?"

"We need to know."

"I don't."

"Fran..."

Her eyes burrowed into his tiny brain: "You're never going to stop, are you?"

He looked at her and said, "No."

"Alright, I'll go." Then she laughed fully. "Don't die."

Fran's laugh was like nothing else. The throaty "dreeeee" was her trying to suppress the main event. The laugh sounded like she was gasping for air with silly, high-pitched noises. The best of laughs – the laugh of a beautiful maniac.

Hussy laid back and listened and smiled. As she walked off, he mirrored her laugh with his quiet laugh... and he fell asleep within seconds of the door clicking shut.

He imagined water. He watched the sheen of the surface. There was a little wind and an almost imperceptible tide. But as the light bounced off the top of the water, he knew there was so much life and death down there. Stupid, silly, unfair death on a staggering scale. The silt and sand carried it away, and no-one gave two hoots about something they had no control over.

It only took an hour for Fran to return, but he felt every second swimming in the nonsense.

Hussy knew he was close to drowning.

48

He asked: "Did the D.A. know anything?"

Fran's face contorted at that: "Y'know, I think he knows nothing about everything." Then she smiled at Hussy, still laying on his sofa. "It's quite a skill if you think about it."

"I haven't thanked you yet," he said. "For the other stuff."

Francesca smiled: "It was pretty gross."

"Well," Hussy said. "Thanks."

"Does that mean I finally get that raise?"

"Fran," he said, before another instinctive rub of his forehead and a regret at rubbing between his eyebrows. "I felt like I was going to die."

"Do you want some grub?"

"Eggs would be good. Boiled." He grinned: "Hard."

"Stop saying cheesy stuff... This is real, you lunatic."

"How's my suit?"

"Crusty and torn. I think it's a goner."

"Damn."

"I have some spare."

"I don't think I'm your size."

She held out her index finger: "You want me to prod your gob to shut you up?"

He could feel the welt on his face. He always looked so ugly, but now he knew he must look like roadkill.

"Nah," and he stared at her. His eyes slammed shut and he fell into a dreamless sleep.

It must have been for the merest of time. It felt like five minutes but it could have been five days.

It didn't matter, he woke with a smile and Francesca was still there. She was wearing a different outfit. A white t-shirt, hip-hugger jeans, but still with her beautiful brown skin.

She was washing him. His face, his chest. He said: "Don't."

Fran said: "How you see yourself is not how others see you."

"Then they're not seeing the truth."

Fran pondered that, then said: "Who does?"

That made him smile his crooked smile. A couple of poached eggs sat on a plate with some wholemeal toast.

Francesca grinned and her broad, beautiful smile that would stay with him until the end of his life.

"Eat," she said.

"Good eggs," he loved the buttery feel of the yokes sliding down.

She laughed and said: "I laid them myself."

"Thanks, Fran," then Hussy fell asleep again.

Now it was school... oh God, why was it school again? He berated himself for repetition but these dreams kept coming.

He had become a librarian instead of a prefect at school. Both unpaid roles were open, but he couldn't resist taking the stranger one.

He remembered the beautiful black girl carve the name of her lover on her arm in the library with a pair of compasses.

He had said it flatly, although it was something so wrong for her to do: "What are you doing?"

She had grinned: "Creating a memory."

She was a librarian too, and she proudly showed him the strange tattoo as it healed and calloused over the weeks after it.

"You still with him?" Hussy had asked.

"Nope."

Then she grabbed his hand and pulled it over the ridges of the scar. It was interesting... the grooves of her beautiful skin.

She smiled as he asked her: "You regret it?"

She said: "Nope!"

49

Hussy awoke and felt around his jaw. It was skinnier, but still tough. No pain, just that sense of dehydration.

Narcoleptic

There was water next to him in a rounded glass. He sipped, gagged for a split-second, then finished it.

He wanted to clean himself, and he flexed his legs in anticipation of getting up. He stroked the bandaged wounds on his face and the pain was minimal.

He smiled wide when he saw Francesca had left an envelope with an "x" written on it. The tiniest show of affection...

The message inside said: *"I went to work! Heard of it?"* She had large and neat handwriting: *"I'll pick up your meds while I'm there and check your messages. Won't be long. Don't get up unless you have to. Luv, FRAN x"*

Luv, eh?

He could go through Fran's stuff, or he could go to sleep. His brain decided he wanted a new dream to begin instead...

Hussy was checking out some shops. He was dressed in a Hawaiian shirt and Bermuda shorts. Francesca was with him. She was wearing pink sweater that wasn't too feminine and blue jeans that hugged and met the sweater low on the waist. She was wearing white trainers and looked as athletic as ever.

They stopped at some shop with a big glass window.

Fran asked: "What were you thinking about when you got those clothes?"

"I don't know." He scratched his head again: "Suicide?"

He liked the suit in the window. It was grey and featureless, something that would help him disappear.

As he pointed, Fran laughed: "The man that time forgot!"

They walked on. Other people were there, but they could walk right through them and they dissipated into the air.

Another shop window and another pause. A disgusting green coat that looked like it was built for an Arctic expedition.

"What about that? Pretty cool," Fran said.

"Fashion is to convince yourself of what you are." Then Hussy's eyes bulged: "WHAT THE HELL IS THAT?"

Some... *thing* was stirring behind the big coat.

"It's a coat, you tit."

"THAT!" It crawled out. Five and a half foot tall, with blazing red hair, and it was SMILING. "It's BARING ITS FANGS at me." The creature was female – it had to be. It was somehow beautiful, some version of a woman, with breasts and hips and wild hair, but it moved on all four of its limbs.

"What?" Fran said. "There's nothing there."

The smiling, beautiful, horrific creature took its right clawed hand and started laughing.

"IT'S THERE!" Hussy said.

The smoky people turned to look, but their voices were incoherent nonsense. No-one looked at the window, they just stared at Hussy.

"THERE! THERE!" He was pointing but no-one else seemed to see anything.

"Stop it, Steve," Fran whispered. "Everyone's looking. Do you need your meds?"

"IT'S TRYING TO BREAK THROUGH THE WINDOW." The

creature dragged down its claws on the window. The nails on its imaginary chalkboard made it laugh even more. "CAN'T YOU HEAR THAT?"

"STOP IT." Now Fran stared at him and stroked his face. "There's nothing there."

He watched the creature take its right forefinger and draw a large circle on the glass. It had blue eyes... why would something like that have blue eyes?

"Fran!" Hussy turned to run away. The scratch of the glass... No, no.

"It's ok," she said, and there was genuine love there. "Don't look," and she put his hands over his eyes, but he opened them as soon as he heard the glass on the window shatter.

Hussy pulled at Fran's hand but she wouldn't move.

"STEVE!" Her face contorted: "Stop it!"

He started to run. He looked back and Fran put her head onto one side. The creature ran through her, and all Fran did was shout: "STEVE" and she was fine... her smoke form fitting beautifully together again and shouting: "OH, COME ON!"

Hussy stood still and watched the creature sit down on four legs and smile. It flexed its muscles and licked its lips.

Then he turned and ran again. He charged through crowds of people and they exploded into dust as he did. But, as he looked over his shoulder, Fran still remained solid and frozen with a slight smile, as the creature prowled forward slowly.

Hussy charged into an ice cream bar and slammed the

door behind him. The bell tinkled, and the guy behind the counter was decked out in a white suit. He had a thin, long face, a big chin with a tuft on hair on the end. He was so damn tall too, 6'10"? More?

"Hello," Hussy said.

The irregular man smiled: "Hello."

The giant flicked his finger, and it lit into a small flame. He then scooped into the white ice cream marked VANILLA and licked it off his forefinger.

"And, gee," the giant said, "you're a boneee-fideee pervert." Then he smiled his too long smile and silently reached under the bar and passed Hussy a shotgun.

Hussy said: "What's this?"

"It isssss what it isssss, and gee, sometimes a see-gar is just a see-gar." He had a thick raspy voice that loved the s's and c's.

"A cigar?"

"Sssso get out there and sssort thissss out."

Now his smile was terrifying. Some twisted version of the creature outside.

Hussy backed towards the door, heard the tinkle of the door as he opened the door and faced the outside.

In the clouds, he heard the claws slightly scraping at the pavement. He shot at the sound and the kickback was immense. He flew backwards and laid stunned on the ground. The blonde version of Fran was then over him, stroking his head gently. She said: "Iz ok..." Then he shut his eyes again.

When he opened his eyes again, Hussy was sitting in a small, comfy seat. He was in an audience. They were performing something on the stage. A lot of men and women were standing around saying "Good grief" to each other. The men were in suits, and the women were in sexy dresses and short skirts. Again, their words were impossible to decipher.

Hussy was on the left hand aisle. He looked to his right, and Fran was there in an evening gown that couldn't decide what colour or shape it was. But now she looked like herself again.

"I love you," he said to her.

"I don't believe you." She kept watching the show.

"Why?"

"You always seem to be naked," she said. "It's disgusting."

And then he was naked.

"Classic anxiety dream," Hussy said.

"Yeah? I don't believe you."

"You said that before. And I still love you."

"You're getting dull. Do I have to liven everything up? Do you want me to talk backwards? Do the funky chicken?"

"Why?"

Then she faced him: "The world is just not for you."

He could hear ringing in amongst the nonsense. He returned to his sanguine self: "What's that?"

"Ringing, you idiot," Fran laughed, "Wake up and leave me alone."

50

Why don't you believe?

Hussy laughed a rare laugh: "I have to now."

Peter poured him another glass of red wine. He did it with a smile that Hussy didn't like: *Come now, why didn't you believe there was something more?*

Hussy thought and said: "I don't..." he corrected himself: "*didn't* feel a part of whole." Then he paused as Peter watched him. "I never felt the need to be part of a community." He downed the wine: "When everyone fits in, nothing progresses."

And did you progress anything?

Hussy had nothing to say in return to that.

You know the rules on such incidents...

"Wasn't Jesus Christ's death a suicide? Or a homicide from God?"

It doesn't work like that.

"Why?"

Peter poured a glass of wine for himself: *Because...*

It was the first time Peter had stumbled for words. He repeated: *Because...*

"And you don't think there are easier ways to make a point?"

Peter stumbled, then: *People remember death.*

"Like they've remembered the billions of people that have died before?"

It's all... academic in the end.

Hussy drained the final glass. "Ok," he said. "I'm ready now."

51

Hussy woke up and answered the phone. "Hey."

"Hey you. It's Fran. How're you doing?"

He withheld the desire to laugh: "I've been asleep."

"I've got your meds, ok?"

"Ok."

"Do you think you'll be able to move if I help you?"

"Yes."

"We'll stop by the hospital first to check you out."

"I don't need a doctor."

"Yes, you do." Now her laugh made a tinkling sound like the door in his nightmare. "Don't make me hurt you!"

But he laughed too. "Ok, Fran."

"Y'know, I just had an argument with some Lieutenant."

"Marcus?"

"Yeah... He wants to see you. He says it's urgent. He wouldn't take no for an answer. I knocked him down to 4pm."

Hussy looked down at his bruised, bloodied and scarred torso. "I still need something to wear."

"I thought of that. Your room is locked. I could buy

something quick. There must be a charity place somewhere near..."

"There's a key stuck under the second drawer of my desk."

"Steve... you never let ANYONE in your room..."

"There are no booby traps and there's my other suit..."

"*Other* suit?"

"Why do you think I always look the same?"

"I..."

"It's in the wardrobe. Some shirts. Take whatever money we'll need."

"Money?"

"It'll be there."

"Steve?"

"Still here."

"You sound weird."

That confused him: "I always sound like this."

"I'll be back soon, ok?"

"Ok."

Hussy placed the receiver back quickly.

He got up and tested his body out. He staggered then laid down again... minutes of breathing and staring at the ceiling.

He felt trapped. An institutionalised loner. A lifelong, twenty-five year stretch in mental solitary confinement, whose routine – like his body – had been broken a little too much.

52

Once he was confident he could stand, Hussy wandered to the window of Fran's bedroom and looked out of it.

All of the hail had dissolved, but the streetlight was still there. The sun was out and the lawn looked very green.

He missed the shimmering glisten of ice. Like water, he liked the thoughts of what secrets were hidden below.

He explored around Fran's place. The apartment was neat with no ostentation. Eleven DVDs on the shelving units, all good choices. A dozen books, no beauty magazines, and sweet impressionist paintings on the walls.

Hussy wandered on like that for a half hour or so. And no clues to anything at all other than what he'd always thought about Fran. He drew personal lines at opening drawers or wardrobes but he knew they'd contain nothing shocking. She was far too smart for that.

All of it went in circles. He couldn't rationalise things he didn't know about. Hussy had enough trouble rationalising things he did know about. The wondering wanderer. The wandering wonderer...

He closed his mouth again and sat on the settee and fell into a dreamless sleep.

Fran poked him awake: "HEY! What're you doing up?"

"Just thinking."

Fran said: "You look like ****!" She put her arms around

him to hold him steady as she led him to the bedroom. "Here..."

"I can still walk," he said, but he didn't stop her.

She rested him down on her double bed.

"Here ya go." She pulled the clothes out of the bag and the meds out of her pocket.

"Thanks."

"I'll get you some water." She went to get up.

"I don't like you running around like this for me."

"Remind me never to give you a gift. You'd probably kill yourself." She got some water from the kitchen. She brought a little mirror with her too. "This is AFTER I cleaned you up."

She gently unwrapped his bandages. His face had collected colours. His nose was broken flat, and his puffed up lips had a faint green stain around them. His cheeks and forehead were purple and cut and the cuts had black in them. Hussy's chin had little grey-pink flaps of skin that hung off red goo. On the flaps, he found it interesting he could still see the stubble.

There wasn't much left of his face. Only the strange blue eyes peered out, half open but still watching and recording life.

"Some people would say this was an improvement." Then he laughed at his joke. A boxer, a road-crash victim, whatever...

Francesca waited for a reaction, but he didn't show any.

"I'd better get dressed," and he took his meds.

"New bandages first." Fran said and she tried to smile as she asked: "Want to go to the hospital now?"

53

The wait lasted four hours in Accident and Emergency.

Fran goofed around to keep him entertained. She could also read his mind: "Why do you drink so much?"

He paused and smiled: "How did you know?"

"Smell," she said matter-of-factly. "Your voice doesn't change... but it's on your breath and in your pores."

Hussy laughed a little at that: "You're a better detective than me."

Fran shoved his arm, smiled and said: "I know!"

Hussy said: "Why don't you drink?"

"Meds."

"What for?"

"Oh," and now Fran was the one eager to change the subject, "manic depression."

Hussy looked at a face that glowed with happiness almost all of the time: "You'd be the last person I'd think would suffer from that..."

Fran said: "I'm a better actress than I thought."

"Fran... Anyone with brains gets depressed."

"I know." Fran paused again, then: "We're quite the pair. Mr. Snoozy and Me."

Hussy tilted his head as he looked at her, and she blushed and turned away.

Fran said: "Wanna hear a story?"

"Always," Hussy replied. Whatever medication he'd taken had made her face somehow more beautiful than ever, and shift slightly before his eyes. Her attitude sent out light.

She tapped him on the nose: "WAKE UP!"

"I'm ok."

"Steve," she said. "I drank loads of booze last week."

"I thought you couldn't..."

"I needed to see." Then she smiled her beautiful smile, but something tinged with sadness in her eyes.

"Ok."

"And I knew I couldn't drive home, so I walked, and then when I got back to my place, I couldn't even get the key in the lock."

"Fran..."

"And I poked and prodded at it, and eventually got in," she said, almost earnestly. "But I needed to puke so badly."

Vomit is never shocking to a drinker. Hussy said: "Let it loose on the pavement..."

"Nah," she said, "but when I got inside I puked chunks into my l'il waste-paper bin. But you know what?"

Hussy looked at her: "I don't."

"It was made out of wicker... like woven willow. And all the puke dribbled out on my hands."

She started laughing and Hussy just kept looking.

Francesca liked the strange expression of Hussy's face.

"Let's cheer up and play The Fight Game," she said.

"Huh?"

She looked around the Accident and Emergency room. There was a man with a bruised face being consoled by his pretty lover. The result of a late night bar fight? A middle aged woman had her breast almost escaping from a hospital dressing gown...

Francesca looked at Hussy, and he was drawn in by her eyes. He could swear they had turned green. Fran said: "You pick the three people you want if we have a fight with each other."

"Ah..."

That made her laugh. "Think about who's toughest and smartest and most likely to kill."

"Ok."

And so they did.

Hussy picked the three oddest looking people. The gal in the dressing gown, another with a limp that vomited in front of them – making them hide laughs as they raised their feet. Then he picked the oldest of the lot. Maybe 90, being berated by the staff because he kept wanting to light a cigarette inside.

Fran picked the old man too, but the other two were pretty and young. The curly-haired girlfriend of the guy whose face was torn up. A muscle-bound guy in shorts and a sling on his right arm.

They continued to laugh as they fictionalised this fight.

For the first time in a long time, Hussy was able to stay fully awake and never feel sleep overcoming him. He was happy.

54

Hussy watched the bulky 14" TV floating above the room while Fran scooted off to find a toilet. The rolling news was running along the bottom of the screen. "Two women found dead," as the reporters continued to analyse the latest Iraq War and the legalities of Blair's policies.

Politics always bored Hussy. He knew he was a grain of sand with precisely one vote. A non-entity incapable of becoming anything more.

He shut his eyes and wished he could shut his ears too.

Fran returned from the toilet and prodded his forehead to wake him up. The room glistened again, just like her smile and her beautiful skin.

"Wake up, sleepyhead."

Fran laughed, never looking up at the screen on the wall.

Hussy never looked up either, for fear of drawing attention to the horror.

He was led into triage with Francesca helping him through.

"You done so well, pretty lady!" A cheery little Filipino nurse said, directing the praise to Fran.

"I, like, started training to be a physio when I was younger." Fran beamed. "Iz fun!"

A doctor came in and he prodded around Hussy's face.

"Ow."

Narcoleptic

"Sorry, mate."

Then he poked around his ribs.

Hussy said, flatly: "Ow."

"No need to mess about with x-rays," he said in a Brummie accent, "your nose is broken. Coupla ribs are too." Dr. Ray went on: "You'll be fine, mate. We'll get you sorted."

They gave Hussy 57 stitches, lots of irrigation, some fresh bandages, tape on his nose, ah-ing about his throat being burnt on the inside, silly steri-strips around the cuts, and some powder to settle his stomach that he never found time to take.

The blood test indicated he was still heavily drunk and that his liver was working overload.

When Fran looked concerned, he massaged the bottom right of his torso and said: "Lucy Liver is doing her job!"

She laughed and gripped his hand. Oh, God, he was so happy...

Then, of course then, Marcus showed up. The toupee was back on his head, and Francesca couldn't take her eyes off it.

"Hey, toup," Hussy said.

Marcus made out like he hadn't heard that. "What happened to you?" There was genuine concern in his voice.

"Got into a fight. You should see the other guys."

"Was this last night?"

"Yeah."

"Do you have witnesses?"

"Why?"

"Does your... woman... have to be here?"

"You can talk to me directly," said Francesca.

Marcus sucked on a molar at the back of his flabby mouth, the phoniest of gestures.

"We found Jenny's body last night."

Fran said: "WHAT?"

"Jen and some old lady in the apartment near Rick's." Marcus stared at Hussy: "Yes, indeed."

Hussy pulled his hand over his head.

"Jenny was in Rick's place," and Marcus's eyes almost had something like enjoyment in what he was saying, "she'd been shot in the head. Same with the lady..."

Hussy looked deeply at Marcus, who scratched the back of his toupee. He could see it, see the way he moved his eyes so gently to the side.

Hussy started: "You're a damn li..."

"SO," Fran nudged him and interrupted. She was right to. "Did you find anything inside their places?" she asked.

"No," Marcus now looked embarrassed. Maybe he didn't like lying?

Hussy's booze-addled cogs started to turn as Marcus said: "I just thought you'd want to know about it..."

Hussy looked at him and watched as Marcus turned away then flicked back his gaze. It still looked dubious.

Hussy said: "Someone's trying to tell us to back off."

Then Marcus stared at him: "I don't know... Will you?"

"No."

"You need to learn to keep your mouth shut, Hussy."

And, then, the strangest of things. Marcus's eyes softened for an instant and he said earnestly: "Be careful, I'll call you tomorrow and you better answer..."

55

Hussy was woken up by Bogey licking his face... that strange rasp of a cat's tongue.

"Hullo!" Fran said and grinned wildly.

"Hello," Hussy replied, and let Bogey nestle into his chest. Bogey fell asleep immediately and Hussy stroked his head idly.

"You've got the knack," Fran said.

"I'm knackered," and he felt his ribs almost as a show, "but it's ok."

"Jesus, Fran, what happened?"

"You feel asleep when they wrapped your ribs."

"And you stayed here?"

"Don't get excited... I slept on the couch."

"You didn't have to do this..."

She prodded his forehead: "I did."

Fran sat down on the edge of the bed slowly, careful not to disturb Bogey.

She said, all wide eyes: "Whatchu actually know?"

"Very little about anything."

She prodded his arm, again careful not to wake Bogey, "About Rick."

"Ah, I'll work it out." Hussy's voice was emotionless.

"But will ya?" Her face crinkled into concern.

Hussy liked the feel of Bogey's breath on him. They always say that cats – any animal – can lull people to relaxation.

Fran sat close to him on the bed, and the heat of that almost made him withdraw. But it was so beautiful, broken ribs and all. He knew, he knew, but he was so happy.

"Stop thinking too much," Fran said, then, with a change of emotion something like sorrow, "And you're doing too much."

And Hussy replied: "And that happens all too often," as he turned his neck with his right hand and it sounded with an audible crack. Bogey's eyes flicked open, but then shut again.

He sank his head back on the pillow but he knew sleep wouldn't come now.

Too much speed, too many uppers and not enough booze.

But that was ok. He was ready.

After Fran left, he drank a half-bottle of vodka over a couple of hours. Fortified, he went to Rick's apartment building.

The floors were scrupulously clean, very different from before. No stickiness on his soles. He knocked on the doors on the ground floor, holding up his silly detective's license. The picture made him look like an inflated corpse.

There was no response, other than some suspicion of

Narcoleptic

peepholes scratching open. Two times he felt he heard that sound.

He creaked up the stairs again.

The door opened to the old woman's apartment once again.

Another woman looked out. She said: "Oh, Steve..."

Hussy shut his eyes, then opened them and walked in anyway: "Hey, Fran."

She didn't even lift the gun from her side.

He walked past her and slumped on the sofa, hoping that the plants would kill him properly this time.

The room stank of bleach and Hussy said: "You know the thing that annoys me the most?"

"Steve..."

"The fact they're treating you like a cleaner."

"She was an informant, y'know?" Fran started.

Hussy sat with his hands open in front of himself. Death held absolutely no fear for him. And Fran was the finest human being he'd even known. This magical creature.

Her face locked as she said: "Rick knew way too much. When we found out he knew too much it had to happen."

"Fran... We?"

That made her smile: "Oh, stop it. You don't even care about the full story."

And that made him smile: "Not really."

"Rick was a horrible person, wasn't he?"

Narcoleptic

"He was," Hussy said: "Was Ms. Pearson?"

Fran tapped the gun against her thigh and rubbed around her eye with her free hand: "She certainly wasn't an angel."

Hussy kept looking at her.

Fran said: "You know, don't you? All of it?"

"Yeah," and Hussy shrugged and smiled. "I'm actually getting pretty good at this job."

"Oh, stop it," Fran smiled back and gripped the gun.

"It's ok," Hussy said. "I'm ready for this."

Fran said: "I'm so sorry."

"I can't say I blame you," Hussy said. "But Rick didn't do those things to the kids, right?"

"No, it was all when he found out there were some who were 16 or 17. And they *weren't* kids."

"Fran..." and now he felt anger.

"You know he paid to have sex with me when I was 18?"

"Fran..."

"You know what he called me before I shot him?"

"Fran... this is..."

Fran stared at him, then raised her gun: "DARK MEAT."

"Does that make it ok to cull idiots?"

"You know he SMILED when he said it?" Fran tapped her gun against her forehead: "Jenny knew too much as well. The..."

"Cops," Hussy said, "were in on the whole thing."

She sighed: "And Wilson..."

"Yeah, Fran, I worked that out too."

Her face blurred and twisted: "You don't know anything. There was..." She lowered her gun and kissed his forehead: "You don't understand how the world works, do you?"

"The women were too young, Fran."

"16, 17, 18." She said the numbers with reticence. "It wasn't even *that* illegal. It was, it was... *controlled.*"

The gun was so small it was almost laughable to Hussy. Then he shook his head and refocused on Fran. He wasn't scared. In an odd way, this was the ending he had always wanted.

"That's a little gun," he said and opened his bloodshot eyes wide. That minuscule thing couldn't kill him.

He looked at Fran and she fully looked at him for the last few minutes of his life. "Y'know, you aren't even ugly."

When she smiled, Hussy said: "Thanks."

Fran spread her hand over Hussy's face and kneaded his forehead. Something like sanity took over him.

It was the most wonderful feeling of his life: "Fran..."

"Sometimes it was NICE, ok?" Her voice raised: "Even some of the old geezers. It was, it was..."

Hussy shut his eyes: "You were still a kid..."

He could hear her irritation: "It wasn't even illegal."

"I know... it's just the organisation of it." Hussy tried to formulate some thought: "Knowing you got the job with me just to scout Rick..."

"I knew no-one could ever hurt me," she said as she tapped her gun on her knee. "I would have... Tyrone would have..."

Hussy opened his eyes and said, simply: "Francesca."

Now her eyes blazed: "Who are you to judge?"

That made Hussy laugh: "I'm nothing."

Francesca shouted: "But you ARE something! You're as messed up as everyone else!" The gun was still low against the curve of her hip: "SAY HOW YOU FEEL!"

Hussy looked up at Fran and said: "I feel it's not right."

"The killings?"

Hussy knew he was going to die, so he shrugged and said: "All of it. It's just wrong."

She placed her left hand on his forehead again: "Say why."

"You killed a 16-year-old kid."

"I didn't," her eyes started to hang. "Bishop was an idiot. You know he's dead now? Tyrone dealt with him..."

"But you knew what Bishop did. You protected it."

"Steve... You don't know everything. You don't..." She rubbed her hand through his hair. "Just forget everything, ok?"

The feeling was incredibly soothing, but as he kept his eyes shut he said: "I can't. It'll be with me when I'm asleep." He tilted his head: "My brain needs to be aired out anyway..."

Fran rested the gun against his forehead. He could have reached up, spun her around and wrenched it out of her hand. But he didn't want to. She had far more importance in the world.

"I'm ready," he smiled. "At least gimme a kiss on the lips."

Fran whispered: "Not so pious now, huh?"

She kissed him on the lips and it was the most beautiful experience of a wasted life. He said: "Hmm."

Fran said: "You sly dog," and Hussy heard her say: "I love you" a second before the sharp yet soft sound of a silenced gunshot made him fell asleep.

56

The waves of serenity lapping over Hussy's brain were broken by the taste of blood. He woke up and saw Fran with the gun still in her hand. Her eyes were shut and her face was as unchanged and as beautiful as always. Her mouth was formed into an O shape and behind her were the contents of her head.

For a minute, he stared at her. His stupid mouth gaped open. He looked at a lost, beautiful human being. He hadn't pulled the trigger but his intractable mind had caused her death.

He looked at his watch. It was three hours later. Then the tears came, why hadn't they before?

Fran's grip had solidified on the gun. Hussy brushed back her hair, then – as gently as possible – he cracked back her fingers to release the gun.

He carried her body to the bed and rested Ms. Pearson's sheets over her head.

He walked back to the office, thoughts pounding away for an hour as he took extended slugs of vodka from the plastic bottle in his pocket.

Once inside, Hussy deleted all of the files on the investigation from both his and Acton's computers. Then he shredded all of the files he could find.

All of that took another two hours, as Hussy supped vodka to try and dull his senses through the whirring sound of everything being turned into meaningless strips.

Then he looked out of the window of his office. All these people dashing about... where were they going to? They all knew where they were going to end up...

The world was this unfair mess filled with stupid people doing stupid things.

When beauty existed – true beauty filled with intelligence and courage and insight – it was nullified or destroyed by cowards at an early age.

He called 999 and told them Fran had killed herself. He gave them the address and said nothing more.

Then Hussy sat on his chair, surrounded by his world of DVDs and books and music. He finished off the vodka, put his gun in his mouth, pulled the trigger and fell asleep for the last time.

57

"So I'm actually dead?"

Yes.

Hussy rubbed his temple, trying to replicate Fran's touch. "I think I killed them," Hussy said. "Was I asleep when I did it?"

You weren't.

"That poor old lady... even Jenny," he kneaded his head and all of the scars had disappeared: "And I basically killed Fran."

The barman looked at Hussy steadfastly and said: *You didn't kill anyone. We merely had to know how you felt.*

There was no reason for Hussy to say anything now.

He sensed the kindness in Peter's eyes as he said: *We'll make sure the right thing is done... just give up the vodka, ok?*

Peter clicked his fingers and it sounded like a clap of thunder.

That sound was replaced by a finger poking his head and saying: "Poink, Poink, Poink," over and over.

Hussy lifted up his head from a strange brown desk, and he looked at the woman. She was partly Fran, but in complete negative. He remembered her from his hallucinations. She was shorter, with blonde hair, larger breasts, green eyes and pale skin. A wondrous, smiling, pocket rocket in a white t-shirt, trainers and hip-hugger jeans.

He knew immediately that she must be protected no matter what...

"Fran?" he murmured. This time he would do it right. He would, he would...

The woman grinned: "It's Ally."

Hussy rubbed his eyes with his right hand. He turned the

hand in front of himself, but it looked the same as always. He said: "Well, at least I got a vowel right."

They were in a black cave. The walls of the cave had alien pictures and alien words. *Mise-en-scene, Diegesis, Chiaroscuro, Cinematography, Film Noir, Expressionism, Zeitgeist, Plagiarism, Cyberpunk, Connotation,* and more, more, more.

"Steve," Ally laughed, "dey're gettin' fuggin' restless out dere!"

"Who?" Was this what heaven was like? Or hell?

She poked a finger at the door: "Dem!"

There were noises – murmured, complaining human voices – outside. There was a door, and young adults peered through a small frame of reinforced glass in the centre of it.

Ally beamed a smile as bright as Fran's: "Tara's holdin' 'em back!"

Hussy's mind disassembled then reassembled: "Al..." he said, knowing this couldn't be hell if Ally was there.

She said "C'mon!" and then danced on the spot and sang to the theme of The Conga: "Doot, doot, doot... dis is my bum now!" She spun around and touched her toes: "Toot, toot, toot... now I'm gonna fart!"

Hussy blew a raspberry and then said: "Fuck it, Al." He laughed: "Bring on the masses..."

Hussy shut his eyes again.

His mouth beamed the broadest of smiles, as he waited for the truth to begin again.

Printed in Poland
by Amazon Fulfillment
Poland Sp. z o.o., Wrocław